KENJI MIYAZAWA (1896-1933) has been compared to Lewis Carroll, Hans Christian Andersen and the Brothers Grimm, but his profound compassion, stemming from his Buddhist faith and his scientific background, makes him that unique combination of East and West that symbolises Japan's great gifts to the world. A dedicated vegetarian (a rarity even in today's Japan) and a staunch believer in animal rights mark him as a pioneer of his time and a writer who speaks directly to the greatest concerns of the twenty-first century.

ROGER PULVERS is an author, playwright, theatre/film director and translator. His novels include *The Death of Urashima Taro*, *General Yamashita's Treasure*, *Star Sand*, *Liv*, *The Dream of Lafcadio Hearn*, *Half of Each Other*, and *Peaceful Circumstances*. He has also published numerous works of nonfiction, collected essays and translations from Japanese, Russian and Polish. Roger's plays have been performed extensively in Australia, Japan and the U.S. He has twice directed at the Adelaide Festival of Arts in Australia and at major theaters in Japan. He was assistant to director Oshima Nagisa on *Merry Christmas, Mr. Lawrence*. In 2016 he wrote the screenplay for and directed the film of *Star Sand*, which was released throughout Japan in 2017. Prizes and honours include the Crystal Simorgh Prize for Best Script at the 27th Fajr International Film Festival in Tehran, the Miyazawa Kenji Prize and the Noma Award for the Translation of Japanese Literature. In 2018 he was awarded the Order of the Rising Sun, and in 2019 the Order of Australia.

ALSO BY ROGER PULVERS

*Liv*

*Half of Each Other*

*The Honey and the Fires*

*The Dream of Lafcadio Hearn*

*Peaceful Circumstances*

*The Unmaking of an American*

*My Japan*

# NIGHT ON THE MILKY WAY TRAIN

*and nine other stories*

# KENJI MIYAZAWA

# NIGHT ON THE MILKY WAY TRAIN

*and nine other stories*

*translated from the Japanese by*

# ROGER PULVERS

BALESTIER PRESS
LONDON · SINGAPORE

Balestier Press
Centurion House, London TW18 4AX
www.balestier.com

*Night on the Milky Way Train and Nine Other Stories*
Original text in the Japanese by Kenji Miyazawa
Original titles: 銀河鉄道の夜, セロ弾きのゴーシュ,
注文の多い料理店, マグノリアの木, インドラの網, オツベルと象,
グスコーブドリの伝記, フランドン農学校の豚, 雪渡り, よだかの星



A CIP catalogue record for this book
is available from the British Library.

ISBN 978 1 911221 85 2

Cover illustration by Alice Pulvers



This book is a work of fiction. The literary perceptions and
insights are based on experience, all names, characters, places,
and incidents either are products of the author's imagination
or are used fictitiously.

# CONTENTS

# Night on the Milky Way Train

## A LESSON IN THE AFTERNOON

'So you see, boys and girls, that is why some have called it a river, while others see a giant trace left by a stream of milk. But does anyone know what really makes up this hazy-white region in the sky?'

The teacher pointed up and down the smoky white zone of the Milky Way that ran across a huge black starmap suspended from the top of the blackboard. He was asking everybody in the class.

Campanella raised his hand, and at that, four or five others also volunteered. Giovanni was about to raise his hand, but suddenly changed his mind.

Giovanni was almost sure that it was all just made up of stars. He had read that in a magazine. But lately Giovanni was sleepy in class nearly every day, had no time to read books and no books to read, and felt, for some reason, that he couldn't properly follow anything anymore.

The teacher noticed this instantly.

'Giovanni, you know what it is, don't you?'

Giovanni stood up courageously. But once on his feet, he wasn't able to give a clear answer. Zanelli, sitting in the seat in front of him, turned around and snickered at him.

Giovanni was flustered, blushing from one ear to the other.

The teacher spoke once again.

'If you were to take a close look at the Milky Way through a big telescope, what would you find it made of?'

Giovanni was now absolutely sure that you'd find stars, but just like the moment before, he couldn't get his answer out.

The teacher, perplexed, finally turned his gaze to Campanella.

'Well, what about you, Campanella?'

Campanella, who had raised his hand so readily a moment before, just stood in his place fidgeting, unable to answer the question.

The teacher, now more surprised than ever, stared for some time at him.

'All right, then, I'll do it,' he hastened to say, pointing to the starmap. 'When you look at this hazy-white Milky Way through a good big telescope, the blur is resolved into a great number of tiny stars. Isn't that right, Giovanni?'

Giovanni, now red as a beet, nodded, and before he knew it his eyes were filled with tears and he thought ...

*That's right, I knew it all along, and so does Campanella, because it was all in a magazine that we once read together at Campanella's father's house, and he's a scholar!*

*Campanella leafed through that magazine and then went straight into his father's library, brought a thick book from the shelf, opened it to MILKY WAY, and we spent forever together looking at the lovely photograph of white specks that covered the pitch-black page.*

*The reason why Campanella didn't answer the teacher right away, even though there was no reason at all for him to forget, is because he feels sorry for me because I have to work hard before and after school and then I feel too down-in-the-dumps to play with everybody or even to talk with him very much.*

When Giovanni thought about how Campanella had deliberately not answered out of sympathy for him, he felt indescribably sad both for himself and for Campanella.

The teacher began again.

'So, if we think of the Milky Way as a Celestial River, then each and every one of these tiny little stars may be seen to be a grain of sand or pebble on the bed of that river. If we imagine it to be a giant stream of milk, then it's even more like a river, and the stars become minute fatty globules floating inside the white liquid.

'Now, ask yourself, what does this liquid actually do, and you will see that it transmits light at a given speed through the void of space, and our Sun and Earth are both floating inside it too. So, you see, we are all living in the liquid of the Celestial River, and when we gaze out from where we are, just as water appears bluest at its deepest spots, so will the places with the most stars look to us the whitest and haziest. That is where the sky's riverbed is the densest and most far reaching. Now look at this model.'

The teacher pointed to a large lens that was convex on both sides. Inside the lens were countless grains of sand, all glistening and gleaming.

'This closely resembles the shape of the Milky Way. You can think of all these glittering grains of sand as stars, all radiating their own light just as our Sun does. Our Sun lies some distance from the centre to the edge, and the Earth is not far away. Now imagine yourself inside this lens at night, looking out. Through this thinner part of the lens you will see only a few grains—stars, I mean—shining.

'But if you look in this direction and in this one, where the glass is thickest, you will see any number of shining grains—stars, I mean— and the farther you look directly into it, the more blurry and milky-white everything will appear. That is how we see the Milky Way today. As for the actual size of the lens and the various stars inside it, class time is over now so we'll discuss it all again in our next science lesson.

'And as tonight is the Milky Way Festival, I hope that you will all go outside later and take a good close look at the sky. That's all. Please put away your books and notebooks.'

For a while the whole classroom was filled with the sounds of books being stacked and desktops being creaked open and slammed shut. In a moment all stood up as straight as arrows, bowed to the teacher and left.

# THE PRINTING HOUSE

As Giovanni was walking out the school gate, seven or eight children from his class were gathering in the yard, forming a circle around Campanella by the cherry blossom tree in the corner. They were no doubt meeting to discuss how to get the big snake gourds they needed to put lights into and float down the river for the star festival that night.

Giovanni hurried out the gate waving his arms. He passed by many houses where people were busily preparing for the Milky Way Festival, hanging decorative bulbs made of yew tree needles from their eaves and fixing lights to the branches of cypress trees.

Without stopping off at home, he turned three corners, entered a large printing house, greeted the man in a baggy white shirt doing accounts by the door, removed his shoes, stepped onto the wooden floor and opened the big door in front of him. Inside all the lights were on even though it was still afternoon, rotary presses were clacking and clanging away, and lots of people with cloth tied around their head or visors perched over their eyes were reading or counting in singsongs and hums.

Giovanni went directly to the man who was sitting at the tall, third desk from the door and bowed to him.

The man rummaged about on one of his shelves for a moment and handed Giovanni a sheet of paper.

'This'd be the amount you might be able to pick,' he said.

Giovanni pulled out a small flat box from the foot of the man's desk and went to a spot in a well-lit corner of the room, squatting down beside cases of type propped against the wall. He began to pick tiny type, no larger than grains of millet, with a pair of tweezers.

'Hey, Three-Eyes!' said a man in a blue apron passing behind him.

Several men nearby chuckled coldly without saying a word or so much as looking at him.

Giovanni painstakingly picked all his type, rubbing his eyes over and over again.

Some time after the clock chimed six, having thoroughly compared the flat box full of type with the sheet of paper in his hand, he returned to the man at the tall desk. The man took the box, giving him a slight silent nod. Giovanni bowed, opened the door and went back to the accountant dressed in white who, also without uttering a sound, handed him one little silver coin.

At this Giovanni's face suddenly lit up, he bowed to the accountant in the highest of spirits, took his satchel from the foot of his desk and darted for the door.

From there, whistling cheerfully, he stopped in at the bread shop, bought a small loaf of bread and a bagful of sugar lumps, then sprinted off as fast as his feet would take him.


# HOME


THE LITTLE HOUSE THAT GIOVANNI CAME HOME TO IN SUCH HIGH spirits was the left one in a row of three located off a back street. Purple kale and asparagus plants were growing in a wooden box beside the door, and shades were rolled down over two little windows.

'I'm back, Mum!' said Giovanni, slipping out of his shoes. 'Are you feeling all right?'

'Oh Giovanni, you must have worked so hard today. It has been cool today and I have been feeling just fine.'

Giovanni stepped up from the entryway onto the floor. His mother was resting in the front room with a white cloth over her face.

'I bought some sugar lumps today, Mum,' he said, opening one of the windows. 'I wanted to put a few in your milk for you.'

'You eat first, dear. I don't feel like it just now.'

'Mum, what time did Sis go back?'

'Oh, around three, I think. She did everything for me.'

'Your milk hasn't come, has it?'

'It should have by now,' she said.

'I'll go get it for you.'

'Don't hurry on my account. You go ahead and eat something first, Giovanni. Your sister cut up some tomatoes and left them there.'

'I'll have them then,' said Giovanni, taking the plate of tomatoes sitting by the window. 'Mum, I'm sure dad will be coming home soon now,' he added, munching hungrily on the tomatoes and a piece of bread.

'Yes, I think so too. But why are you so sure?'

'Because it said in this morning's paper that the catch up in the north was really great.'

'But, you know, your father may not have gone fishing up there.'

'No, he's out there all right. Dad couldn't have done anything bad enough that they had to send him to prison or something for. It wasn't all that long ago that he came to our school and donated all those things like that huge crab shell and those reindeer horns. They're still keeping them in the specimen room. All the sixth-year pupils get to see them when the teacher brings them one at a time to the classroom. Year before last, on a school excursion....'

'Your father promised to bring you back an otter coat the next time he came back, didn't he?'

'All the kids make fun of me about that every time they see me.'

'Do they say nasty things to you?'

'Yeah, except for Campanella. He never says nasty things. Whenever somebody does, he always looks really sorry for me.'

'Your father and Campanella's father were close friends just like you two when they were little.'

'Oh, that's why dad used to take me sometimes to Campanella's house. Everything was so good then. I used to go lots of times on my way home from school. They had a train that ran on an alcohol burner. When you hooked up seven rails it made a circle with telegraph poles and signals, and the train could only go when the signal light turned green. Once we ran out of alcohol so we put in some kerosene, but the little boiler got all sooty.'

'Did it now....'

'It's always so quiet there when I pass by every morning delivering the paper.'

'That's because it's still early.'

'They've got a dog named Sauer and he's got a tail just like a broom. He yelps and sniffs and when I'm there he follows me all the way to the end of the street. Sometimes he even follows me further. Tonight everybody's going to make lanterns out of snake gourds and float them down the river. I'll bet anything that dog will follow us.'

'That's right, tonight was the Milky Way Festival.'

'Uh-huh. I'll go get your milk and have a look on the way back.'

'All right, you do that. But don't go on the river, Giovanni.'

'I'll just watch from the bank. I'll only be gone an hour.'

'You don't have to come back so soon. I'm not worried so long as you're with Campanella.'

'Oh, we'll be together all right. Should I close the window for you, Mum?'

'Well, let me see ... it's already getting cool now, I suppose.'

Giovanni rose, closed the window, and put away his plate and the remaining bread.

'Then I'll be back in an hour and a half,' he said, whipping his shoes on.

He passed through the dark doorway.

# NIGHT OF THE CENTAUR FESTIVAL

WITH HIS LIPS PUCKERED AS IF HE WAS WHISTLING SOME SAD SONG, Giovanni came walking towards town, down a slope that was a pitch-black tunnel of thickly growing cypresses.

A single tall street lamp, radiating a brilliant yet soft light, stood at the foot of the slope. As he made his way steadily towards the lamp, his shadow, which had been trailing behind him like a lanky blurry murky ghost, became darker and more distinct, kicking up its legs and swinging its arms until turning around to his side.

*I'm a great locomotive! I'm speeding up here because this is an incline. I'm going to pass that lamppost any second now. Hey, now my shadow's the needle of a compass. It's gone around in a circle and now it's right in front of me!*

That is what Giovanni was thinking as he took giant steps beneath the street lamp. Just then Zanelli, who had sniggered at him in class that day, came out of a dark alleyway on the other side of the post. He was wearing a new shirt with pointed collars, and he all but collided with Giovanni as their paths crossed.

Giovanni was about to say, 'Zanelli, are you going to the river to float gourds?' But before he could get the words out, Zanelli hollered nastily from behind, 'Giovanni's getting an otter coat from his father!'

Giovanni's heart suddenly went cold and he heard a ringing in his ears coming from all around him.

'Who do you think you are, Zanelli!' he screamed back. But Zanelli had already disappeared into a house with a cypress tree in front.

*Why does he keep saying those things when I haven't done  anything to him? He looks just like a rat when he runs away like that. He's so stupid, that's his problem!*

Giovanni's mind was leaping from one thing to another as he passed through town with all the houses decorated in the most beautiful array of ornamented branches and lights.

The watchmaker's shop had a radiant fluorescent light in the window and an owl, made of stone, whose red eyes rolled around every second. All kinds of jewels were piled on a platter made of thick glass the colour of the sea. The platter rotated, revolving the starlike jewels and bringing a copper centaur around from the other side. Between the centaur and the jewels there was a circular black map of the heavens decorated with blue asparagus leaves.

Giovanni forgot himself in the map of the heavens.

It was much much smaller than the star chart that he had seen at school earlier that day. But with this one all you had to do was to set the date and time by turning the platter, and the sky for that night would appear in the oval opening. The Milky Way ran straight through the middle, a smoky zone of white stretching from one end to the other with what looked like steamy vapours rising, as if after an explosion, from the bottom reaches.

In the depths of the shop stood a small telescope on a glowing yellow tripod and behind that, on the back wall, hung a big map depicting the entire sky in constellations of bizarre beasts, snakes, fish and bottle shapes. Giovanni wondered if the sky was really so crammed with scorpions and brave warriors and things, and he thought, standing there in a daze ...

*Ah, I'd like nothing more than to travel inside there as far as a human could go!*

Then suddenly he remembered the milk for his mother and he walked away from the watchmaker's shop. He went through town swinging his arms and deliberately straining to swell up his chest, even though the shoulders of his coat were pinching him.

The air was crystal clear, flowing through the streets and past the shops as if it was water. Street lamps were tucked away amongst the blue branches of fir and oak, and the six plane trees in front of the Electric Company, decked inside, outside and everywhere with miniature light bulbs, made the whole place look like Mermaid City under the sea.

All of the children, dressed in freshly pressed kimonos, were running about, shouting and whistling the tune of 'Once Around the Stars'.

'O Centaurus, Let the Dew Fall!'

As they played happily, fireworks of blue magnesium burned in the sky.

But Giovanni, his head drooping down, was lost in thoughts far away from that lively atmosphere about him. He hurried in the direction of the dairy.

He found himself on the edge of town where countless poplar trees stood as if floating up into the starry sky. He opened the darkened gate of the dairy and waited by the dusky kitchen, which smelled of cows.

'Good evening,' he called out, removing his cap.

It looked quiet inside, and there wasn't a soul in sight.

'Good evening,' he called loudly again, standing up very straight. 'Anybody home?'

After a while an old woman shuffled out. She did not look well at all, and mumbled to herself, 'What d'ya want?'

'Um, we didn't get any milk at my place today,' said Giovanni in a spirited voice, 'so I'm here to fetch it.'

The old woman scratched a patch of skin under her red eye and looked down at Giovanni.

'No one around here now, and I dunno. Come back tomorrow,' she said.

'But my mum's sick, so we must have it by tonight.'

'Well, in that case come back a little later.'

The old woman was almost gone when Giovanni called out, 'A little later? ... well, thank you!' He bowed and left.

When Giovanni was about to turn the corner into town he noticed six or seven boys in front of the grocer's on the road to the bridge. Their black shapes mingled with their dimly glowing white shirts. They were each carrying a lighted gourd lantern, whistling and laughing.

There was no mistaking those whistles and laughs. They belonged to Giovanni's classmates. At first Giovanni, startled, started to turn back, but then he changed his mind and headed for the bridge with very sure strides.

'Going to the river?' That's what he wanted to say, but the words got stuck in his throat, and before he could say anything at all, Zanelli hollered.

'Giovanni's getting an otter coat!'

Everyone immediately joined in.

'Giovanni's getting an otter coat!'

Giovanni, blushing to his ears, started to walk. He was already past them when he noticed Campanella standing tall amongst them. Campanella was keeping silent, with a smile of soft compassion on his lips, no doubt worried that Giovanni might take offense at the others' words.

Giovanni avoided Campanella's gaze, and as he left his friend behind he heard the others break out in their loud whistling again. He turned the corner, looking back at them and saw Zanelli looking back too. Campanella, now whistling with all his might, was disappearing into the milky-white haze surrounding the bridge.

Giovanni, overwhelmed by sadness, began to run out of the blue, as all the little children, who thought Giovanni funny as he ran, hopped about on one leg, screaming, yelling and hooting with their hands over their ears.

In an instant he found himself hurrying towards a black hill.

# THE WEATHER STATION PILLAR

Beyond the pasture the hills rolled on one after another, while their flat blackened peaks seemed to be lined up lower than usual, dim and hazy below the Big Dipper in the northern sky.

Giovanni was already deep inside a grove of trees that were dripping with dew. He climbed steadily up a straight and narrow path illuminated by starlight, the single clearing in a thicket of dark plants taking on all shapes and sizes. There were tiny insects gleaming blue amidst the bushes, rendering their leaves transparent blue and reminding him of the snake gourd lanterns all the children had been carrying.

Giovanni came out of the pitch-black pine and oak wood, and all of a sudden there was a vast sky above him, with the Milky Way, soft and blurry white, streaming from south to north.

He could make out the pillar of the weather station at the top of a slope that was a carpet of daisies and bellflowers. Their fragrance was so strong that he felt you could smell it through a dream. A single bird passed over him, crying above the hill.

Giovanni came to the base of the weather station pillar at the very top of the hill and, shuddering, plopped down into the cold grass. The lights of the town below were burning through the darkness as if the town itself was a miniature shrine at the bottom of the sea. He could faintly catch snatches of children's screams and bits of whistles and songs. The wind howled far away and all the hill's plant life rustled. His sweat-soaked shirt started to give him a chill as he looked down on the distant swept-black field from the edge of town.

The sound of a train came to him from the field. It was a little train with a single row of tiny red windows, and inside it all of the passengers were peeling apples, laughing or doing one thing and another. This made Giovanni feel immensely sad, and he once again gazed up at the sky.

But no matter how hard he looked at the sky, he just couldn't see the cold barren place that the teacher had described in class. On the contrary, the more deeply he stared into it, the more he saw a field with little groves of trees and pastures. Then he noticed the blue stars of Lyra, the Harp, multiplying, twinkling all the while, and the Harp itself stretching out its legs then pulling them in until it looked like a long mushroom.

And from where he was down to the town below, everything appeared to be a blurry cluster of countless stars ... or a single vast puff of smoke.


## MILKY WAY STATION


THEN GIOVANNI SAW THE WEATHER STATION PILLAR RIGHT BEHIND him take on the vague shape of a triangular turret, flickering on and off like a firefly. When the blur in his eyes passed, everything became clear and finely outlined, and the turret with its light soared straight up into the dense cobalt-blue field of the sky that was like a sheet of freshly tempered steel. Out of the blue he was sure he heard a strange voice calling ...

'Milky Way Station! Milky Way Station!'

And before his eyes there was a flash flood of intensely bright light, as if billions and billions of phosphorescent cuttlefish had fossilised at their most radiant instant and been plunged into the sky, or as if someone had discovered a hidden cache of precious jewels that the Diamond Company had been hoarding to bolt the price sky high, turning the whole treasure topsy-turvy and lavishing them throughout the heavens. Giovanni found himself rubbing his eyes over and over, blinded by the sudden dazzle.

By the time he came to, he had, for sometime now, been chugging along on the little train. It was really him on the nighttime narrow-gauge railroad, gazing out the window of a wagon with its little row of yellow lights. Inside, the seats, nearly all empty, were covered in blue velvet, and two big brass buttons gleamed on the varnished grey wall opposite him.

Giovanni noticed a tall boy in a glistening jet-black jacket poking his head out the window in the seat directly in front of him. He could have sworn, judging from the boy's shoulders, that he had seen him somewhere before. He wanted to know who it was so much that he couldn't stand it. But just as he was about to stick his own head out his window and take a look, the boy popped his in and turned towards him.

It was Campanella!

Giovanni was about to ask him if he had been on the train from the very beginning, but Campanella spoke up sooner.

'Everybody ran so fast but they missed the train. Even Zanelli ran like mad but he couldn't catch up with me.'

Giovanni thought to himself ... *I got it! We've been asked to go away together.*

But he said, 'Should we wait for them somewhere down the line?'

'Zanelli went home already,' said Campanella. 'His father came to get him.'

Campanella's face turned pale, as if something was hurting him. Giovanni felt funny inside, as though he couldn't remember something that he had somewhere forgotten.

'Oh, gee,' said Campanella, coming alive and peering out the window again. 'I've forgotten my water bottle. And I've forgotten my sketchbook too. Well, no matter, we'll be coming into Swan Station soon. There's nothing I like better than watching swans. I'm sure I'll be able to see them no matter how far down the river they fly.'

Campanella looked down at the round plate-like map in his hand, busily turning it round and round. On the map a single track of rail skirted the left bank of the whitened Milky Way, tracing its way south and further south again. But the really fantastic thing was that the map, a platter black as night itself, was inlaid with little whistle stops and triangular turrets one after the other, and forests and miniature lakes, all shining beautifully in blue, green and bitter orange.

Giovanni was sure he had seen that map somewhere before.

'Where did you buy that map?' he asked. 'It's made of obsidian, isn't it?'

'I got it at Milky Way Station. You mean, you didn't get one too?'

'Gee, I'm not sure if I went through Milky Way Station. We're around here now, aren't we?' said Giovanni, pointing to a place directly north of a sign that read *Swan Station*.

'That's right,' said Campanella. 'Oh, good heavens! I wonder if that dry river bed is just moonlight.'

When the two of them looked they saw the pale bank of the Milky Way glittering with pampas grass growing all along it, rustling and swishing, rolling in the wind into billows of waves in a silver sky.

'That's not moonlight,' said Giovanni. 'It's shining because it's the Milky Way!'

Giovanni felt so elated, he wanted to jump up and down. He tapped his feet, poked his head out the window and, standing as tall as he could on tiptoes, whistled the tune of 'Once Around the Stars'.

He couldn't get a clear picture of the water in the river no matter how hard he looked at it. He kept staring and staring until he gradually saw that the clear water was even more crystal than glass, even more transparent than hydrogen. Maybe it was just his eyes, but the water in spots seemed to be making delicate purple ripples or glimmering rainbows of light as it flowed steadily, silently along. Phosphorescent triangular turrets, perfectly erect, patched the sky.

The faraway turrets were small, the closer ones large; the faraway ones distinctly yellow and bitter orange, the closer ones pale and faintly hazy. Some turrets were triangular, others rectangular; some the shape of chains, others the shape of lightning. But they were all in lines, flooding the field with light.

Giovanni felt more excited than he had ever been, and he shook his head for all he was worth. Then, as far and as wide as his eyes could see, the blues and oranges and all the luminescent turrets began to sway and flicker, as if they were alive and breathing themselves.

'I've made it right into the sky's field!' cried Giovanni. He leaned out the window and pointed to the front of the train with his left hand, adding, 'Oh, this train isn't burning coal!'

'Must run on alcohol or electricity,' said Campanella.

The beautiful little train, chugging and clanking its way along the pampas grass that waved in the sky, through the waters of the Milky Way and the glimmering milky-white light of triangulation pillars, was running on its endless journey.

'Oh, gentians are blooming. It's autumn for sure,' said Campanella, pointing out the window.

Magnificent purple gentians, so fine that they might have been carved out of moonstone, grew amongst the closely cropped grass that lined the track.

'Just you watch me hop right out of here, get some of those flowers and jump back on again,' said Giovanni, his heart leaping with excitement.

'Too late,' said Campanella. 'We've left them behind now.'

But no sooner had the words left his lips than had another batch of gentians flashed brightly past them, and then another, and another, cups with yellow at their hearts, gushing, passing in front of their eyes like rainfall … and a row of triangular turrets, some smoky, others burning, rose up, radiant for all the world to see.

## THE NORTHERN CROSS AND PLIOCENE COAST

'I wonder if my mum will ever forgive me,' said Campanella suddenly, stammering and flurried, but nonetheless resolute.

Giovanni was lost in his thoughts ...

*Sure, that's it! My mum is far down there by the orange-colored turret that looks like a speck of dust. She's thinking about me this instant.*

'I'd go to the ends of the earth to make my mum happy,' said Campanella, doing his best to hold back the tears. 'But I just can't figure out what would make her happiest.'

'At least there's nothing at all wrong with your mum,' exclaimed Giovanni, somewhat taken aback.

'Oh, I dunno. It's just that, I mean, people create happiness when they do something good. That's why I'm sure my mum will forgive me.'

Campanella looked like he had really made up his mind about something.

All at once, the inside of the wagon was flooded with a bright white light. Outside, where the water was flowing without sound or shape over the bed of the glittering river as if diamonds and dew from the grass had congealed on it, there was an island bathed in an aura of pale light. Atop the island, on a plateau, stood a cross, silent and eternal, so dazzling and white that it might have been cast from frozen Arctic clouds, crowned with a pure halo of gold.

'Hallelujah! Hallelujah!'

Voices came from the front and back. The two boys looked around to see passengers in the wagon, the folds of their robes hanging down perfectly straight, some clutching black Bibles to their chest, others with crystal rosaries around their neck, clasping their hands in prayer, all facing the cross outside.

Both boys found themselves rising to their feet. Campanella's cheeks gleamed like ripe apples.

The island and the cross moved gradually back down the line. The far bank of the Milky Way glowed through the mist, the pampas grass fluttered as if someone was breathing on it, the silver air was momentarily opaque with smoke, and the countless gentians vanished in the grass then reappeared like gentle will-o'-the-wisps.

But it wasn't long before clusters of pampas grass eclipsed the space between the river and the train, and they caught glimpses of Swan Island now far back in the distance, like a little picture, until the pampas grass rustled and swished once again, and the island disappeared entirely from view.

Behind Giovanni stood a tall Catholic nun he had not seen come on the train. She was dressed in black, and her perfectly round green eyes stared downward as she appeared to be listening humbly to a voice or words coming from the outside. The passengers returned to their seats in silence, while the two boys quietly exchanged words in a sad mood they had not felt before.

'We'll be at Swan Station any minute now, I guess.'

'Yeah, we'll pull in at eleven o'clock on the button.'

Before long, green signals and milky-white posts were flashing by the window, the dark lights of automatic switches, glowing indistinctly like sulphurous flames, passed on back, and the train gradually eased its pace, as a row of electric lights, perfectly spaced, appeared on a platform. The space between the lights became larger and larger, and the two boys came to a stop directly in front of the huge clock at Swan Station.

Two hands of blue tempered steel pointed precisely to eleven on the bracing autumn face of the clock. All the other passengers alighted together, leaving the wagon deserted.

A sign below the clock read ...

> TWENTY MINUTE STOPOVER

'Should we get off here too?' asked Giovanni.

'Yeah, let's!'

The two sprang up at once, flew out the door and made a mad dash for the ticket gate. But all they found at the gate was a bright purple electric light. There wasn't a soul around, not even a stationmaster or someone who resembled a redcap.

The boys came out onto a small square enclosed by gingko trees that looked hand carved of quartz. A wide road led from the square straight off into the bluish light of the Milky Way.

The people from the train seemed to have gone somewhere and vanished. Giovanni and Campanella started up the white road, shoulder to shoulder, casting shadows in all directions like two pillars in a room with windows on all sides or like the spokes of a wheel. Before they knew it they had reached the beautiful riverbed that they had seen from the train.

Campanella put a handful of sand into his palm and grated it with his fingers.

'This sand is all made up of crystals,' he said as if in a dream. 'There's a tiny fire burning inside each and every grain.'

'Yeah!' exclaimed Giovanni, fairly sure that he had learned that somewhere.

All of the small stones on the bed were transparent, no doubt made up of quartz or topaz, some of them crumpled and folded in on themselves, others of corundum giving off a pale misty light from their facets. Giovanni ran straight for the water's edge and dipped his hand into the liquid. The mysterious water of the Milky Way was even clearer than hydrogen and the boys were convinced that it was flowing, because when their wrists were submerged in it they appeared to be floating as if in mercury, and the phosphorescent waves frothed and sparkled as they splashed against their skin.

Upstream, below a cliff that was blanketed in pampas grass, they caught sight of a stretch of white rock, as flat as a sports ground, following the course of the river. They could see the small figures of a number of people who seemed to be excavating or burying something as they stood up and stooped down with some sort of  tool glinting from time to time in their hands.

'Let's go take a look,' said the two boys nearly in unison as they ran for the cliff.

A shiny smooth ceramic nameplate stood at the entrance to the area of white rock ...

THE PLIOCENE COAST

Slim iron handrails had been planted in spots on the opposite bank, with lovely wooden benches sitting by them in the sand.

'Hey, I found something weird,' said Campanella puzzled, stopping to pick up what looked like a long narrow black walnut with pointy ends.

'It's a walnut! Look, they're all over the place, probably carried along by the river. They're in the rock too!'

'They're big for walnuts. This one's twice as big as normal. And this one's in perfect shape.'

'Let's go over where the people are right now. I bet they're digging up something or other.'

The two boys went ahead holding their jaggedy black walnuts. To their left the ripples glowed against the water's edge like dim lightning, while to their right tufts of pampas grass, as if fashioned of silver or mother-of-pearl, blanketed the cliff face, swaying and rolling.

Once close enough to get a good look, they saw a tall scholarly man in boots and terribly thick glasses writing busily in a notebook. He was quite beside himself giving instructions to three assistants who were swinging pickaxes or shoveling with scoops.

'Don't break up that protuberance, use a scoop, a scoop! Watch out, dig around it first. No, not that way! No, no, go easy with it, will ya?'

The massive pale skeleton of a beast protruded from the soft white rock. A good half of it had already been excavated. It was crushed on its side. The rock itself, which bore two cloven hoof prints, had been carefully carved out into some ten numbered squares.

'You fellows here to inspect?' asked the scholarly man, twinkling his glasses. 'You saw all those walnuts, didn't you? They'd be somewhere in the neighbourhood of, oh, 1,200,000 years old, I'd say. Not very old, when you come down to it. This place here was a coastline some 1,200,000 years back, just about after the Tertiary Period. Plenty of shells under here too. Saltwater ebbed and flowed here where the river is now. Now, take this beast here. We geologists call it a "bos" ... hey, you, put down that pick! Can't you be more careful and use a chisel? This bos was the ancestor of today's cow. This place, I'd say, would've been literally crawling with them.'

'Are you going to make a specimen out of it?'

'No, we need this as evidence. You see, we know this place to be a magnificent thick stratum, and we've got all the proof we need that it was formed 1,200,000 years ago. But some others don't see it in  that light, claiming that it might be just wind, water or empty sky. Follow? However ... hey, you, don't use your scoop on that! There's bound to be a set of ribs buried under there.'

The professor scurried over to the dig.

'It's time,' said Campanella, checking his wristwatch with the map. 'Let's go.'

'Well, I am afraid that we must take our leave,' said Giovanni, bowing formally to the professor.

'Must you? Well, goodbye then,' he said, rushing helter-skelter about and supervising things right and left.

As for the boys, they ran for their lives back over the white rock so as not to miss the train. They found themselves running just like the wind without skipping a single breath or getting hot sore knees.

*If we can run like this, we can run anywhere in the whole wide world!*

That's what Giovanni thought as they passed by the river bed. The light on the ticket gate gradually grew larger and larger, and, in a flash, they were back in their old seats looking out the window at the very place they had been not a moment ago.

# THE BIRDCATCHER

'Mind if I sit down here?'

Giovanni and Campanella heard a kindly, gravelly adult's voice behind them.

The voice had come from a man with a stoop and a red beard, dressed in a shaggy brown overcoat and carrying a huge bundle wrapped in white cloth and slung in two equal halves over his shoulders.

'Fine with us,' said Giovanni in reply, shrugging.

The man smiled faintly through his beard and lifted his bundle carefully onto the baggage rack above.

Giovanni was feeling immensely sad and lonely as he stared in silence at the clock in front of him. Far up ahead what sounded like  a glass flute rang out and the train moved smoothly forward. Campanella was examining the ceiling. A black beetle had come to rest on one of the lights, casting a monstrous shadow. The man with the red beard was staring intently at the two boys and smiling, as if something was taking him back to somewhere or some time else. The train gradually began to pick up speed, and the pampas grass and river alternated in lighting up the air outside.

'May I enquire as to where you boys would be heading?' asked the man timidly.

'Further than anybody,' answered Giovanni sheepishly.

'That's really something. That's precisely where this train is going.'

'So where are you going?' asked Campanella suddenly in a quarreling tone that made Giovanni smile.

Then a man across the aisle, sporting a pointy cap and dangling a large key from his waist, stole a look at them and smiled too, making Campanella blush and smile himself. But the man with the red beard didn't look angry in the least.

'I'm gettin' off a bit down the track,' he said with his cheeks twitching. 'Birdcatchin's my line.'

'What birds do you catch?'

'Why, cranes an' wild geese. An' herons an' swans, too.'

'Are there lots of cranes here?'

'Masses. They were just yelpin' back there, didn't ya hear 'em?'

'No.'

'If ya listen you can still hear 'em now. Prick up your ears and listen.'

Giovanni and Campanella raised their eyes and listened carefully. Amidst the soft echo of the chugging of the train and the swishing of the pampas grass they heard the bubbly frothing and gurgling of water.

'How do you catch a crane?'

'Do you mean cranes or herons?'

'Uh, herons,' said Giovanni, not really caring which.

'Easy as pie! Herons are made of congealed sand from the Milky Way's bed, an' they keep comin' back to the river in a constant stream. If you wait on the bank all of them come soarin' down with their feet out like this, an' I pluck 'em off like sittin' ducks just before they reach the ground. Then they curdle up and pass on serenely to, well, greener pastures. Everybody knows what happens next. You press 'em.'

'Press 'em? You mean like flowers or specimens?'

'They're not specimens, no. I mean, everybody eats 'em. You boys know that much, don't you?'

'Sounds funny to me,' said Campanella, cocking his head.

'Good heavens, it ain't funny an' it ain't dubious in the least. Watch.' The man stood up and brought his bundle down from the rack, untying it with a nimble twirl of his fingers.

'Feast your eyes! A fresh batch.'

'They really are herons!' blurted out the boys.

There were some ten of them, somewhat flattened down, their black legs crumpled in under them, lying in a row side by side as if carved in relief, their pure white bodies radiating the very light of the Northern

Cross that they had passed.

'They've all got their eyes closed,' said Campanella, gently touching a bird's white eyelid that was the shape of a crescent moon. They even had white feathers like spears on their heads.

'See what I mean?' said the birdcatcher, wrapping up his catch again, folding the cloth and securing it with twine.

*Who on earth around here would eat a heron?*

This is what Giovanni thought as he asked, 'Do herons taste good?'

'Good as goose! I've got orders flyin' in faster than I can fill 'em. But the wild geese, I should say, are in greater demand. Geese have much more breeding, an' what's more, they cause no trouble in the handling. Here.'

The birdcatcher untied the other bundle. Inside it was a row of yellow, off-white and speckled geese with their beaks lined up neatly and their bodies slightly flattened out, just like the herons.

'These geese may be gobbled anytime. How about it? Dig in.'

The birdcatcher gently pulled the yellow leg of a goose. It came off in a nice clean piece, as if made of chocolate.

'Eh, how about it? Have a piece on me,' he said, breaking the leg in two and giving them a half each.

Giovanni took a little bite and thought to himself ...

*Hold on, this is cake! It even tastes better than chocolate. This man is pulling our leg when he says that these geese can fly. He's just a cake salesman out in the field somewhere. But I do feel sorry for him, taking his cake and eating it too.*

But even so, he didn't stop munching away.

'Have another bite,' said the birdcatcher, reaching again for his bundle.

'Thank you just the same,' declined Giovanni, who really did want to have another piece.

So the birdcatcher offered it to the man with the large key in the seat across the aisle from him.

'Much obliged, but I shouldn't really be dippin' into your stock,' said the man, tipping his cap.

'Don't mention it,' said the birdcatcher, adding, 'Well, how're things goin' in the world of migratory birds?'

'Great, we're runnin' at full capacity. Just day before yesterday, during the second shift, calls kept comin' in askin' me why the light in the lighthouse was on the blink, blinkin' at irregular intervals, you know, so I says to 'em, heaven only knows, it's not my doin', but it's the birds migratin' in big packed flocks passin' in front of the light, so what can you do? Ain't no good come complainin' to me, I tell 'em, take your complaint, I says, to the big fella with the long narrow beak an' the spindly legs, the one wearin' the cape that flutters in the wind! I gave it to 'em, I did! Ha!'

The pampas grass was gone now leaving the field outside shining with a new radiance.

'What makes the herons so hard to handle?' Campanella had been meaning to ask this from before.

'Look,' said the birdcatcher, turning back to the boys, 'you see, if you want to eat a heron, you've gotta first hang him up for a good ten days in the liquid light of the Milky Way, or you can bury 'em in the sand for a few days. It evaporates the mercury and then you can eat 'em.'

'This is no bird, it's really cake, isn't it!'

Both Giovanni and Campanella had been thinking this, but it was Campanella who had taken the plunge and come out with it.

'That's right, this is where I get off,' said the birdcatcher, looking in a frightful tizzy. He then stood up, grabbed his big cloth bundle and, in a flash, was nowhere to be seen.

The boys looked at each other, their eyes saying, 'Where did he go?' But the lighthouse keeper was all grin, leaning in front of the boys to peer out their window.

Out there they all saw the very same birdcatcher who had been with them a moment before. He was standing on a riverbank surrounded by chickweed that was giving off a lovely yellow and eggshell-white phosphorescence. He was staring up at the sky with a determined look, his two arms stretched out like wings.

'There he is! It's so weird. I bet he's got his eye on the birds right now. If only they would fly down before the train goes by!'

No sooner had those words left Giovanni's mouth than did a veritable snowfall of herons, squawking and calling, come fluttering down from the barren dark violet sky. At that, the birdcatcher, chuckling with glee that things were really coming his way now, spread out his legs on a sixty-degree angle, taking in the birds by their black legs hand over fist and pinning them down in his cloth bag. Once inside the bag the birds flickered blue, on and off like fireflies, until, in the end, they turned a hazy white colour and shut their eyes.

Most of the birds, however, were not caught. They came to a safe landing on top of the sand by the river, and as their feet touched the sand their bodies curled in, flattening like melted snow, spreading along the surface like molten copper fresh from a blast furnace, their forms clinging momentarily to the sand, turning light and dark, light and dark, until finally blending in without a trace.

The birdcatcher, now with some twenty birds in his bag, suddenly lifted both arms skywards, like a soldier who had been hit by a bullet and was on his last legs ... when, in a flash, there was no sign of him outside and Giovanni heard a familiar voice coming from the seat next to him.

'Ah, I feel like a new man. Yep, nothin' like a hard day's work, best way to earn a crust!'

It was the birdcatcher himself, making rows of the herons he had just caught and stacking them in neat piles.

'How did you get back here all at once?' asked Giovanni, feeling both that he had expected the man to do it and yet that it was something quite miraculous as well.

'How? 'Cause I wanted to, that's how. Now, where on earth was it you two boys said you hailed from?'

Giovanni was about to answer when he realised that he couldn't for the life of him recall where in the world he had come from. Campanella, too, had turned bright red trying to remember.

'Well, from a long, long way off, anyway,' said the birdcatcher, nodding as if he knew all about it.


# GIOVANNI'S TICKET


'WE ARE ABOUT TO LEAVE SWAN ZONE. SEE FOR YOURSELF. THERE'S the renowned Albireo Observatory.'

Outside the window, four big black buildings stood in the very middle of the Milky Way, which itself was a galaxy of fireworks. Two enormous spheres, of translucent blue sapphire and dazzling yellow topaz invisibly looped together, were revolving around each other on the flat roof of one of the buildings. When the yellow one made its way around back, the smaller blue one circled forward until their edges overlapped, forming a single, exquisite, green convex lens-like shape. Then gradually the centre would bulge and the blue sapphire would appear exactly in front, a green sphere with a yellow topaz ring around it. Again, slowly, the sapphire would move across to the other edge, reversing the shape of the lens before, and the two would part company as the topaz came forward. The black observatory buildings lay there silently, as if at rest, encircled in the  formless, soundless liquid of the Milky Way.

'That's an instrument for measuring the speed of the water as it flows. You see, the water....'

That was all the birdcatcher could say before, without warning, a tall conductor in a red cap came up to their seats.

'Please have your tickets ready,' he said.

The birdcatcher pulled a small slip of paper from his inside pocket without saying a word. The conductor glanced at it, immediately turning to Giovanni and Campanella, wagging his finger and pointing to them, as if to say, 'And where are your tickets?'

'Oh, gee,' said Giovanni, fidgeting at a loss for what to do. But Campanella produced a small grey ticket from out of nowhere, as if by second nature. Giovanni, now in a real flurry, reached deeply into his jacket pocket to see if there was a ticket there, finding a big folded piece of paper. He quickly brought out his hand, surprised himself that there was something in it, and held up a green piece of paper, folded in quarters, about the size of a postcard. He thought ...

*I don't know what this paper is, but the conductor has his hand out, so I may as well hand it to him!*

The conductor took the piece of paper from him, stood at attention and carefully unfolded it. He fiddled with the buttons on his jacket as he read it, while the lighthouse keeper did his best to steal a peek at it from below. Giovanni, quite excited, was sure that the paper was some kind of certificate.

'Have you carried this from the Third Spatial Region?' asked the conductor.

'Search me,' said Giovanni, chuckling and looking up, now feeling considerably relieved and safe.

'Very well. We will be arriving at the Southern Cross in the neighbourhood of the next Third Hour,' said the conductor, returning Giovanni's ticket and proceeding on down the aisle.

Campanella was dying to find out what was written on Giovanni's ticket, so he quickly took a peek at it. Giovanni couldn't wait to see either. But all they could make out on it were designs of black arabesques with ten or so funny-looking printed letters amongst them. They felt that if they continued to stare at the piece of paper they would certainly be swallowed up into it.

'Good heavens,' said the birdcatcher, taking a glimpse from the side. 'That ticket is really tops. It will take you higher than the sky! Even higher. With this ticket you've got safe conduct to anywhere your heart desires to go. With this ticket you can go wherever you wish on the imperfect Four Dimensional Milky Way Dream Train. You boys are really something!'

'Oh, I dunno,' said Giovanni, blushing, folding up his ticket and putting it back in his pocket.

He felt rather awkward as he stared out the window with Campanella, vaguely aware that the birdcatcher was throwing them glances from time to time, as if to say, 'You boys are really tops!'

'We'll be pulling into Eagle Station any moment,' said Campanella, comparing his map with three little pale-white triangular turrets on the opposite bank.

Giovanni, without knowing why, felt indescribably sorry for the birdcatcher, and when he thought about him being so overjoyed at becoming a new man when he caught his herons, wrapping them up in his white cloth bundle or just stealing glances at people's tickets and praising them to the high heavens, he wanted to give him everything he owned, his food and everything, though he really didn't know him very well at all. If it would make the birdcatcher happy, he would even stand for a hundred years at a time in the shining field of the Milky Way and catch his birds for him.

Giovanni couldn't remain silent any longer. 'What is it you wish for more than anything else?' is what he wanted to ask him. But that would be altogether too abrupt. As he considered what else he might ask and turned towards the birdcatcher ... the birdcatcher wasn't there at all! And his huge white bundle was gone from the overhead rack as well.

Giovanni immediately looked outside, sure that he would be out there, his legs planted solidly, searching the skies for a heron to catch. But his broad back and tapered hat were nowhere to be seen. All that was there was a waving white sea of pampas grass and a beautiful blanket of sand.

'Where'd he go off to?' asked Campanella in a daze.

'That's a good question. I wonder where on earth we'll ever meet up with him again. I just wanted to say a few more words to him.'

'Oh, me too.'

'I really feel awful, because at first I thought he was in our way.'

Giovanni had never felt odd in quite that way and certainly had never been able to express it in words.

'Hold on, I smell apples!' said Campanella, looking around in amazement.

'Could it be because I just had apples on my mind? I smell apples too. And Seven Sisters roses!'

Giovanni looked all around, but the smell seemed to be coming from outside the window. This puzzled him all the more because it was autumn and not at all the season for Seven Sisters roses.

Before they knew it a boy about six years old, with glossy hair, wearing an unbuttoned red blazer, was standing nearby. He had a terrible expression of fear on his face, shivering and quaking in bare feet. A young man in a properly fitted black suit, as tall and straight as a zelkova tree blasted for an age by the wind, stood beside the little boy, holding him firmly by the hand.

'Oh God, where are we? Oh, it's so lovely here,' said Kaoru, a little girl of about twelve with pretty brown eyes, wearing a black overcoat and clinging to the young man's arm as she stared outside in wonder.

'Why, it's Lancashire. No, it's the state of Connecticut. No, oh ... we've come to the sky! We're on our way to Heaven,' said the young man in black, radiating good cheer to the little girl. 'See for yourself. That is the sign for Heaven. There's nothing to be afraid of now. We are being summoned by God.'

But then, for some reason, deep furrows appeared on his brow and he looked weary. He tried to force a smile as he sat the little boy down next to Giovanni and gently instructed the girl to sit beside Campanella. She sat down obediently, folding her hands together on her lap.

The little boy had an odd expression on his face. 'I'm going to see my big sister, Kikuyo,' he told the young man, who had just seated himself opposite the lighthouse keeper.

The young man, unable to say a word, stared with the saddest eyes at the little boy's wavy soaking-wet hair. Suddenly the little girl put her hands to her face and sobbed.

'Your father and your sister, Kikuyo, still have lots of work to do,' said the young man. 'But they'll be along someday soon. More than that, just think of how long your mother has been waiting for you. She's waiting and worrying and imagining the songs that her sweet little boy, Tadashi, would be singing. She would be picturing you holding hands with the other children and skipping round and round the elderberry bushes when snow falls in the morning. So let's go right now and see mummy!'

'Okay, but I still would rather have not got on that ship in the first place.'

'I know, but look up. See? That fantastic river, see it? The milky-white place in the sky that you used to see from your window all summer long and sing, *Twinkle, Twinkle, Little Star* ... it's right there! See how lovely it is, shining so brightly?'

The little girl, who had been crying, wiped her eyes with a handkerchief and looked outside.

'We have nothing to be sad about anymore,' explained the young man calmly to them. 'We're travelling through this fine place and soon we will be in God's house, where it will be as bright as bright can be, the smells are sweet and the people are truly grand. All of the people who went in the lifeboats in our place will surely be saved and will go back to their own mothers and fathers who are  so worried about them or to their own homes and children. Now, we'll  be there soon, so cheer up and sing out.'

The young man consoled them, stroking the little boy's wet black hair. Gradually his own expression brightened too.

'Where did you people come from?' asked the lighthouse keeper, finally beginning to catch on. 'What brought you here?'

The young man gave a faraway smile.

'Well, the ship hit an iceberg and sank,' he said. 'Their father was called home unexpectedly two months ago, so we waited and set off later. I was a university student hired as their private tutor. But then, just four days out, today, or maybe, yesterday, the ship hit an iceberg, listed just like that, then began to sink. There was some hazy moonlight that night but the fog was extremely thick. Half of the lifeboats on the port side had gone under and there weren't enough left to carry everyone.

'I realised that in a moment the whole ship would be lost, so I cried out with all my might for somebody to help save these children. The people nearby made a path for them and started to pray, but there were still many little children and their parents standing between us and the lifeboats, and I didn't have the heart to push them aside. Yet, I still felt that it was my duty to save these little ones, so I tried to elbow my way past the children in front.

'Then it dawned on me that, better than saving them in that way, I should bring them just as they are now before God. Then I thought I should save them and take on the entire sin against God by myself. But there was no way for me to do it. It tore me up inside to see mothers going crazy throwing kisses to their children in the lifeboats and fathers standing stiffly on deck holding back their tears.

'I knew that the ship was going down fast, so, resigned to fate, I embraced these two little ones, determined to stay afloat for as long as possible. Someone threw a lifebuoy at us but it slipped and flew way out of reach. I frantically ripped some latticework from the deck and we clung on to it. Suddenly, as if from nowhere, someone was singing a hymn, and soon everyone joined in in many different languages.

'Then we heard a loud boom and we were plunged into the water. I held on tightly to these two, but we must have been caught in a whirlpool because everything vanished and the next thing we knew we found ourselves here. Their mother passed away two years ago now. Oh yes, the lifeboats must have been safely away from the ship when it sank, I mean, what else would you expect with all those seasoned sailors rowing them?'

Faint prayers could be heard, and Giovanni and Campanella, their eyes smarting, recalled things that had slipped out of their mind.

*Oh, I wonder if that big ocean was the Pacific. And someone is working his life away in a far northern corner of that ocean where the icebergs float, battling the wind and the frozen tide and the violent cold in a little boat. I really feel sorry for that man, really sorry! What can I do to make him happy?*

That is what Giovanni thought, his head bowed in grief.

'Who knows what happiness is?' said the lighthouse keeper, comforting him. 'So long as you're on the proper road, no matter how trying a thing may be, you'll be getting closer, one step at a time, up and down the high points and the low points to real happiness.'

'Yes, that's true,' said the young man in a reverential tone. 'To attain the truest happiness you must first know all kinds of sorrow, for such is God's will.'

The little brother and sister, Tadashi and Kaoru, were already sunk deep down into their seats, fast asleep. They now had soft white shoes on their feet where there had been nothing before.

The little train chugged and clanked, making its way along the phosphorescent bank of the river, with fields appearing through the windows on the other side as if in a magic lantern. Hundreds and thousands of triangular turrets of every size stretched to the very edge of the fields, the larger ones topped with red-dotted surveyors' flags so thick and dense that on the horizon they appeared like a pale bank of mist, and from there and from further afield than anyone could see, signal fires and flares of all kinds shot up one after the other into the dark violet sky. The breeze, clear and lovely, was filled with the scent of roses.

'Want one? I bet you've never had apples like these before.'

The lighthouse keeper across the aisle was carefully holding large beautiful golden and red apples in his lap.

'Wow, where'd those come from?' said the young man, genuinely impressed and taken aback. 'They're incredible! I didn't know they had apples like those around here.' He tilted his head, fixing his squinted eyes on the bunch of apples in the man's lap.

'Well, anyway, help yourself. Come on, don't be shy.'

The young man glanced at Giovanni and Campanella, taking an apple for himself.

'And you little tykes there. Come on, come an' get 'em.'

Giovanni didn't much fancy being called a 'little tyke', so he just sat tight in silence. But Campanella thanked the lighthouse keeper. At this the young man took two apples and handed them to the boys. Giovanni rose to his feet and thanked the man too.

The lighthouse keeper, who could now manage to carry the rest of the apples by himself, went to the little brother and sister and gently placed one apple each in their lap.

'Thank you very much,' said the young man looking on. 'Where do they grow apples as lovely as these?'

'Of course this region is farmland, but generally speaking things just grow by themselves. Farming shouldn't break anybody's back. All you do here is sow the seed of your choice and, day by day, the plant grows of its own accord. And the rice here isn't like your rice around the Pacific Ocean, because it's got no husks, and besides, the grains are ten times bigger and they smell absolutely delicious.

'They don't farm up where you're headin', though, but you can eat the apples and cakes there down to the very last morsel, and you'll find yourself giving off a faint sweet aroma through your own pores, a different aroma for each person!'

Suddenly Tadashi blinked his eyes open.

'Oh, I was just dreaming of my mother,' he said. 'She was standing by this great big cupboard or bookshelf or something and she was holding out her hand and looking at me and smiling so big. I said, "Mummy, do you want me to get an apple for you?" And that's when I just woke up. Gee, this is the same train I was on before.'

'You've got an apple,' said the young man. 'This nice man gave us all one.'

'Thank you, sir. Hey, Kaoru's still asleep. I'll wake her up, okay? Sis? Look, we got apples. Wake up and see!'

Kaoru smiled and opened her eyes, rubbing them with both hands from the glare. Then she saw the apples. Tadashi was munching away at an apple as if it was a piece of pie. The peel that he had taken the trouble to peel off took on the shape of a corkscrew as it fell, turned smoky grey, flared and evaporated before reaching the floor.

Giovanni and Campanella stashed their apples in their pockets for safe keeping.

Downstream there was a vast forest growing on the far bank of the river, its thick and deep blue branches loaded down with round ripe fruit, glowing red, a staggeringly tall triangular turret standing in its very centre. The breeze from the forest carried the indescribably beautiful sound of bells and xylophones that mingled with everything, permeating the air.

The young man shuddered, spellbound by the sound.

They all listened to the music in silence as the sky unfolded into what looked like a yellow and light-green meadow or carpet, and pure white dewdrops, like wax, swept across the face of a sun.

'Oh, look at those crows!' cried Kaoru, who was now beside Campanella.

'Those aren't crows, they're magpies,' exclaimed Campanella in what came out as a scolding voice, causing Giovanni to laugh unintentionally and the little girl to feel suddenly awkward.

Black birds in their thousands had come to rest in rows along the milky-white bank, bathing motionlessly in the glow coming off the river.

'Yes, they are magpies,' interceded the young man. 'You can tell by the tuft sticking out of their head.'

By now the tall turret in the blue forest was face to face with the train, and the familiar strains of a hymn's melody could be heard coming from the wagons in the very back. It sounded like it was being sung by a huge chorus of people. The young man turned pale and wan, started to rise and follow the sound, but decided to sit down again.

Kaoru buried her face in her handkerchief and even Giovanni couldn't help but get a bit sniffly. Somehow the melody was picked up by someone, until both Giovanni and Campanella found themselves singing along in unison.

The blue torchwood grove sparkling on the invisible far bank of the celestial river moved gradually back and beyond, whilst the music from the mysterious instruments streaming out of it was almost completely drowned out by the chugging of the train and the rush of the wind.

'Look, a peacock!' cried Tadashi.

'Peacocks, lots of them,' said Kaoru.

Giovanni was watching the reflection of light flickering off the peacocks as they spread and closed their pale feathers above the grove now no bigger than a miniature green shell button.

'Right,' said Campanella to Kaoru. 'It was peacock calls we heard before.'

'Yes, I know,' she said. 'I saw about thirty of them. It was the peacocks that sounded like a harp.'

Giovanni, glum yet not knowing why, wanted to glare at Campanella and say, 'Hey, let's hop off here and have some fun!'

The river divided in two. A turret as high as the sky had been erected on the island at its fork, and on top of it perched a man in a red cap and loosely fitting clothes. He was looking towards the sky and signaling with red and blue flags in his hands.

He waved the red flag repeatedly in the air then suddenly brought it down, hid it behind his back and lifted the blue one as high as he could, waving it furiously, like an orchestra conductor. At that very moment an unbelievable clamour filled the air as if it had suddenly started raining cats and dogs, and whole clusters of little black birds shot, as if out of the mouth a shotgun, across the sky to the far side of the river. Giovanni found himself sticking half his body out the window to get a good look at the tens of thousands of little birds as they flew, each and every one calling through the magnificent dark violet sky.

'Just look at those birds fly,' he said from outside the window.

'Birds?' said Campanella, looking up.

The man in the loose outfit on top of the turret suddenly raised his red flag and waved it madly. At that moment the great cloud of birds froze, an earsplitting crash was heard downstream, and then it turned perfectly quiet. Yet no sooner was there quiet than did the red-capped signaler once again wave his blue flag.

'Now is the time for all migratory birds to migrate! Now is the time for all migratory birds to migrate!' he yelled in a voice as clear as a bell.

And once again the great mass of countless birds shot overhead. Kaoru poked her head out of the same middle window as the two boys, facing upwards with lovely sparkling cheeks.

'Oh, so many birds!' she said to Giovanni. 'And the sky is so pretty too!'

But Giovanni turned a deaf ear to Kaoru, keeping his mouth shut, considering her no more than a big pain in the neck and continuing to look up at the sky.

Kaoru took a faint breath, fell silent and returned to her seat. Campanella, feeling sorry for her, drew his head back inside and concentrated on his map.

'Is that man there to guide the birds?' she asked Campanella faintly.

'He's there giving signals to migrating birds,' he replied, unsure of himself. 'I mean, a flare rockets up or something, telling him to do it.'

Silence filled the wagon. Giovanni wanted to bring his head in from the window, but the bright light inside would be too hard to bear, so he remained as he was and whistled a tune.

*Why am I so forlorn? I should be a kinder person, a more generous person. I can see a small blue flame, hazy with smoke, way beyond the far bank. It is so quiet and cold, but it calms my spirit if I keep my mind on it.*

Giovanni, gazing in the distance, grasped his burning, throbbing head in both hands.

*Is there really nobody who will stick with me to the edges of the universe and beyond? Campanella just sits there jabbering away to that little girl, and it hurts me more than anybody knows.*

Giovanni's eyes filled with tears, making the Milky Way seem even more remote and dreamy white.

By this time the train had veered away from the river, passing above a cliff. The black cliff face on the opposite bank loomed gradually higher and higher at the lower reaches of the river. A huge stand of corn flashed into view, with leaves that were all frizzled and curly and husks that were big and already a striking green, sprouting red hairs and brimming with kernels like pearls.

Soon the number of plants had multiplied until the stand, with plants in rows, lined the area between the cliff and the track.

When Giovanni pulled his head in and looked through the windows across the aisle he saw ears of corn swaying in the breeze, growing all the way to the horizon, laden with red and green dewdrops on the tips of their curly leaves, shining like diamonds that had absorbed the rays of the sun.

'That's corn, isn't it?' said Campanella to Giovanni.

But Giovanni wasn't in a mood to be cheered up and sat there gazing at the field with a moony face.

'Guess so,' he answered.

That's when the train slowed down, passed by a few signals and illuminated switches and came to a halt at a little station.

The pale-white clock face opposite them indicated precisely the Second Hour, the wind died down, the train was still and a pendulum ticktocked the time throughout the still field. Then a faint melody, perfectly in time with the regular ticking of the clock, wafted their way, a thread of sound from the farthest fringe of the field.

'It's the New World Symphony,' said Kaoru to herself.

All the people in the train, including the stately young man in black, were plunged into a tender dream.

*Why can't I cheer myself up in such a peaceful place as this? Why am I so alone? And that Campanella, he's really being mean. We're on this train together and all he does is blabber to that girl. It's really hard to take!*

Giovanni, his face half-buried in his palms, stared out the window on the other side. A flutelike note, clear as glass, rang out and the train began to creep along, as Campanella sadly whistled the tune of 'Once Around the Stars'.

'Precisely, precisely, you see, it's all towering plateaus up here,' blurted out an old man from behind, as if he had just woken up. 'Now, if it's corn you want, you gotta open up a hole two feet deep and plant the seed in that, otherwise you haven't got a prayer.'

'Is that right? I guess we won't be reaching the river for quite some time yet.'

'Precisely, precisely. We're still a good two thousand to six thousand feet above her. We're over one hell of a gorge here.'

It dawned on Giovanni ...

*Sure, we're over the plateaus of Colorado!*

Kaoru, far away in thought, her face like an apple wrapped in silk, was staring in the same direction as Giovanni, while Campanella was still whistling sadly to himself. All of a sudden the corn was gone, leaving a vast black stretch of plain from one horizon to the other.

The New World Symphony was coming in loud and clear from beyond the horizon when an American Indian, an arrow fixed in his little bow, decked out in a white feather headdress and a variety of stones on his arms and breast, started running after the train as fast as his moccasins would take him.

'Gosh, an Indian!' cried Kaoru. 'Look, it's an Indian!'

This woke up the young man in black and sent both Giovanni and Campanella to their feet.

'He's running after us!' she said. 'He's running this way, chasing us!'

'No, he isn't chasing the train,' said the young man, standing up and putting his hands in his pockets and forgetting where he was for the moment. 'He's hunting or doing a dance.'

What he was doing did look very much like a dance. His step was too measured and methodical for a dash. Then, without warning, he stopped dead in his tracks, his white headdress tumbled down in front of him and he fired his arrow quick as a flash into the air. A crane whirled dizzily down and once again he sprinted ahead to catch it in his open arms. He stopped there, beaming.

But his figure standing there holding the crane in his arms and looking in the direction of the train grew steadily smaller and ever distant, two ceramic insulators on a telegraph pole glittered by, and once again they were passing through thickets of corn. The train  was moving along the top of a gigantic cliff, the wide river flowing, shining far down below it.

'Precisely,' said the old man. 'From here on it's all downhill. Which is not to say that it's a breeze gettin' down to river level in one go. This train can never go the other way, 'cause the angle here is too much for her. See, we're pickin' up speed already.'

The train chugged faster and faster down the slope and, as it skirted the very edge of the cliff, the river shone brightly in their eyes. Giovanni's mood brightened too. They sped past a small hut with a solitary little boy standing in front of it. He cried out into the air.

The train was clanking steeply down the incline even faster now, all the people in it pushed back hard against their seats, holding on for dear life. Giovanni and Campanella smiled at each other. The Milky Way was streaming furiously past them, virtually under their nose, giving off brilliant flashes of light. Large wild pinks were in bloom in spots along the pale red bank. The train slowed down by degrees, running steadily and smoothly again. Banners decorated with stars and picks were flying on either bank of the river.

'I wonder what banners those are,' said Giovanni, finally managing to eke out some words.

'Beats me. Nothing like them on my map. There's an iron boat there too.'

'Yeah.'

'Perhaps they're building a bridge,' said Kaoru.

'Sure, they're Army Engineers' banners! They're on bridge-building manoeuvres. Except, I don't see any soldiers around.'

Just then, a little downstream by the opposite bank, the invisible river flashed, and a pillar of water shot up high into the air with an ear-splitting boom.

'They're blasting! They're blasting!' cried Campanella, jumping for joy.

The water in the pillar disappeared, but huge salmon and trout that had been flung into the sky by the explosion remained in the air, their bellies gleaming white as they described a perfect arc before falling back into the river.

Giovanni was in such high spirits now that he wanted to leap into the air himself.

'It's the Army Engineers of the Sky!' he cried. 'Fantastic! Those trout or whatever just went rocketing up like this. I've never been on such a great trip as this. Out of this world!'

'Those trout would be this big close up,' said Campanella. 'This river is just crawling with fish.'

'I wonder if there are little fish too,' said Kaoru, now hooked on the boys' conversation.

'There's bound to be,' replied Giovanni, smiling at her and feeling his old self again. 'If they've got big ones, they'd be bound to have little ones too. We're just too far away to see them.'

'Look, those must be the palaces where the twins live,' exclaimed Tadashi, suddenly pointing out the window.

Two little shrines that might have been fashioned of crystal stood roof to roof on top of a rolling hill to their right.

'What's the palaces where the twins live?'

'Our mother told us about them lots of times,' explained Kaoru. 'There are two little crystal palaces next to each other just as she said there would be.'

'Tell us about them. What are twin stars doing in the sky?'

'Why don't you ask me?' said Tadashi. 'The twins went to the fields to play. Then they had an argument with a crow, see?'

'No, that's not how it went,' said Kaoru. 'Let's see now. It was on the bank of the Milky Way, mummy said so, she ...'

'And the comet came whooshing by. Whoosh! Whoosh!'

'Stop it, Tadashi! That's not the way it was. That's a different story altogether.'

'So it's them playing that flute?' asked Giovanni.

'They're off at sea,' said Tadashi.

'No they're not!' insisted Kaoru. 'They've already been to sea.'

'Yeah I know, I know,' continued Tadashi. 'I can tell you all about it.'

The opposite bank of the invisible river turned red all of a sudden and its waves glittered like needles, throwing willows and everything into stark silhouette. A large crimson fire was blazing in a distant field, its towering smoke threatening to char the deep violet of the sky. The dancing flame was more transparent red than a ruby, more exquisite than lithium.

'I wonder what's causing that fire,' said Giovanni. 'What could be burning to give off a flame as red as that?'

'It's Scorpio's fire,' replied Campanella, his head buried in his map.

'Oh I know about Scorpio's fire,' said Kaoru.

'So what is it then?' asked Giovanni.

'Scorpio burnt to death. My father told me millions of times that the fire burns to this very day.'

'A scorpion's an insect, right?'

'Uh-huh, it is. But it's a nice insect,' said Kaoru.

'A scorpion's not a nice insect! I saw one in alcohol at the museum. It's got a huge stinger on his tail, and the teacher said if it stings you, you die!'

'I know, but it's still a nice insect. My father told me that a long long time ago Scorpio lived in a field in Baldola, and he survived by killing teeny bugs and eating them up. Then one day he was caught by a weasel and it looked like he was going to be eaten up himself. He tried to get away with all his might and he was about to be  pinned down by the weasel when out of the blue there was this well in front of him and he fell right down into it, and there was no way in the world he could get back up, so it looked like he was going to drown for sure. So then he began to pray ...

*"Oh, I can't remember how many living creatures I have killed in my lifetime, but now I found myself trapped by the weasel and running for my own life. Oh, woe is me! Everything is so risky in life. Why didn't I just give my body to the weasel and be done with it? If I had, at least he would have been able to live another day.*

*"Dear God, please look into my heart and in the next life don't throw away my life in vain like this, but use my body for the good and happiness of all!"*

'That's what he said. And Scorpio saw his body turn bright red and ignite into a beautiful flame, lighting up the darkness of the night sky! And he's burning now too, that's what my father said. That fire ... it must be him.'

'Sure, look! The triangular turrets are lined up exactly in the shape of a scorpion.'

Giovanni could clearly see beyond the tower of fire. Three turrets made up a scorpion's front legs, with five others forming the tail with a hook in its stinger. The red flame burned brightly without so much as a crackle.

As the fire receded gradually into the distance, everyone began to hear all sorts of indescribably lively music, to smell what smelled like bouquets of flowers and to hear a mixed murmur of voices and whistling. There appeared to be a town nearby with some sort of festival in progress.

'Oh Centaurus, Let the Dew Fall!' cried Tadashi, who had been fast asleep until then in the seat beside Giovanni.

Outside the window stood a deep blue Christmas tree, a fir or cypress, its branches swimming with countless miniature bulbs, as if a thousand fireflies were swarming throughout them.

'How could I forget? Tonight was the Centaur Festival!'

'Yeah, this must be Centaur Village,' piped in Campanella.

'Momentarily we will arrive at the Southern Cross,' said the young man to the children. 'Please prepare to alight.'

'I'm gonna stay on the train a little bit longer,' said Tadashi.

Kaoru stood up on shaky legs and made preparations to leave. She looked sad to have to say goodbye to Giovanni and Campanella.

'We must get off here,' said the young man to Tadashi, closing his lips firmly.

'I won't! I'm gonna stay on a little longer!'

'You can stay on with us,' said Giovanni, unable to hold himself in. 'We've got a ticket that goes on forever!'

'But we have to get off here,' said Kaoru, sadly. 'This is where you get off to go to Heaven.'

'Who says you have to go to Heaven? My teacher says that we have to create a place that's even better than Heaven.'

'But our mummy's already there, and besides, God says so.'

'A God who says that is a phony God.'

'Your God is the phony one!'

'He is not!'

'What kind of God is your God?' interrupted the young man, smiling.

'How should I know?' said Giovanni. 'But he's not like hers! He's the only real God.'

'Of course the real God is only one,' said the young man.

'I don't mean it that way,' said Giovanni. 'I mean the really real God.'

'That's what I'm saying too. Let us pray that we will all meet someday in the course of time before that real God.'

The young man humbly clasped his hands together, Kaoru did the same, and all of them looked frightfully pale and very reluctant to say goodbye to each other. Giovanni could hardly contain his tears.

'Well now, are you ready? We're nearly at the Southern Cross.'

It was at that instant. Far downstream, there emerged, like a single tree out of the invisible water of the river, a cross studded with lights of blue, bitter orange and every colour under the sun, crowned with a pale white halo of cloud. There was a great hustle and bustle inside the train as all the passengers stood to attention and prayed, just as they had done at the Northern Cross, and cries of joy, like the ones you hear when children reach for floating gourds, were heard, and deep pious sighs.

Eventually the cross came into full view outside the windows with the white halo cloud, whiter than the flesh of an apple, revolving ever so gently around it.

'Hallelujah! Hallelujah!'

Their voices rang out pleasantly in chorus as they heard the crystal-clear call of a bugle from the remotest part of that cold remote sky. The train rolled slowly through a long series of signals and lamppost lights, crawling to an eventual stop directly in front of the cross.

'Well, everyone off!'

The young man took Tadashi's hand, making his way towards the exit.

'Goodbye for now,' said Kaoru to the two boys, looking back at them.

'Goodbye,' said Giovanni in a brusque voice, holding in his tears.

She looked back at them once more, her eyes wide open as if her heart was breaking in two, then silently left. The train was more than half empty, and before they knew it, there wasn't a soul left in it at all. A vacant wind blew through the wagons.

The boys looked outside. All of the people had come together, forming rows in humble prayer, kneeling on the shore of the Milky Way in front of the cross. A holy figure in a white robe was crossing the invisible water, coming towards them with outstretched arms.

But at that very moment, the glass whistle blew, the train inched forward, and a silver mist came streaming up between them and the river. Nothing was visible there now save for a grove of walnut trees, their leaves gleaming, and a cute little electric squirrel with a golden halo who kept poking his face through the mist.

When the mist finally began to lift they could see a wide road lined with electric lights skirting the track for some distance then leading off into the blue. The little pea-coloured lights blipped off as the train approached, as if acknowledging its presence, then blipped back on again as it passed.

The cross had shrunk so small in the distance that it looked like you could pick it right up and hang it on your chest, and there was no way on earth of knowing whether the little girl, the young man and the others were still kneeling on that white shore or had already  gone off somewhere to their heaven.

'Campanella,' said Giovanni, sighing deeply, 'we're alone again. Let's stay together till the ends of the earth, okay? If I could be like that scorpion and do something for the benefit of all people, I wouldn't care if my body burnt up a hundred times over.'

'Me too,' said Campanella, his eyes welling with the clearest tears.

'But what is real happiness, Campanella?'

'Search me,' he answered dreamily.

'We'll keep our spirits up, won't we?' said Giovanni, taking a deep breath and feeling a new strength gushing through him.

'Hey, there's the Coal Sack!' cried Campanella, pointing to a spot in the Milky Way and leaning back as he did so. 'It's a hole in the sky!'

Giovanni was flabbergasted as he peered down into the Coal Sack. It was a huge black gaping hole in the river, and the longer he stared and squinted into it, the more his eyes smarted and he couldn't tell how deep the bottom went or what was down below it.

'I'm not scared of all that dark,' he said. 'I'm going to get to the bottom of everything and find out what will make people happy. We'll go together, Campanella, as far as we can go.'

'Yes we will, Giovanni. Oh,' cried Campanella, pointing to a distant field, 'that's the most beautiful field I have ever seen. Everybody's there. That's the real heaven. Look, my mother's there too. Look!'

Giovanni looked, but what he saw was all milky white and blurry, not at all like what Campanella was describing. He felt indescribably lonely as he peered out, catching sight only of two telegraph poles on the opposite bank, their red crossbeams aligned like linking arms.

'Campanella,' said Giovanni, turning towards him, 'we're going to stick together, okay?'

But there was no Campanella where Campanella had been sitting, only the black shining velvet seat. Giovanni bolted up like a rocket, leaning far out the window so that he wouldn't be heard as he screamed into the sky, pounding his chest hard and crying out with a throat full of tears.

Everything seemed to go black at once.

Giovanni opened his eyes. He had fallen asleep, exhausted, in the grass on the hill. He felt a strange burning sensation inside as cold tears streamed down his cheeks, and he sprang to his feet.

The town below was bound together by countless lights just as before, yet now they were somehow more radiant mellow. The Milky Way, where he had just dreamt himself to, was still a hazy blurry white mass smoking above the black southern horizon, with the red star in Scorpio twinkling beautifully to the right beside it. The stars in the sky did not appear to have changed position very much from before.

Giovanni sprinted down the hill. All he could think of was his mother who was waiting until he came home before having her dinner. He passed through the black grove of pine trees, turned by the faintly white pasture fence and came to the front entrance of the darkened cowshed. It looked like someone was in now, because he saw a cart with two barrels of something loaded on it.

'Hello, anybody here?' shouted Giovanni.

'Coming!'

A man in heavy white pants emerged, adding, 'What can I do for you?'

'Well, we didn't get our milk delivered today.'

'Oh, I'm terribly sorry.'

The man immediately went in back and returned with a bottle of milk.

'Really sorry about this,' he said, handing the bottle to Giovanni and smiling. 'This afternoon I was pretty careless and left the gate to the calf pen open. The little devil made a beeline to his mother and  drank up half her milk.'

'I see. Well, I'll take this home then.'

'Please do. Terribly sorry about this.'

'That's fine.'

Giovanni went out the pasture gate with both hands wrapped around the warm bottle of milk. He walked a distance through a heavily treed part of town, coming out onto the main road, and when he reached the crossroad, he could see to his right the turrets of the big bridge standing tall in the hazy sky over the river where Campanella and the others had gone to float lanterns.

Small groups of women who had gathered on the corners of the crossroad and in front of the shops were looking towards the bridge and speaking in hushed tones. The bridge itself was swimming in all kinds of light.

Giovanni, feeling a strange chill inside, shouted to the people close by, 'Is something wrong?'

'A child has fallen into the water,' said one of them, as they all turned at once towards him.

Giovanni ran for his life towards the bridge. The river was invisible for all of the people on the bridge. A policeman in white was amongst them.

Giovanni reached the end of the bridge and flew down to a wide section of the river. Many lights were moving up and down along the water's edge, and a number of lantern flames could be seen roving the dark embankment on the opposite bank as well. Between them the river, with no lantern to illuminate it now, flowed in a single grey tranquil stream with little more than a murmur. People were standing in a black mass at the farthest point downstream where the river formed a sandbar. Giovanni quickly made his way there, bumping into Marceau, who had been with Campanella earlier.

'Giovanni,' said Marceau, running up. 'Campanella's fallen into the river.'

'Why? When?'

'Zanelli was trying to push a lantern down the river from the boat, and that's when the boat tilted and kind of dumped him into the water. Campanella dove right in after him and he pushed Zanelli back to the boat, and Kato got ahold of him, but then nobody could see Campanella after that.'

'But everybody's looking, aren't they?'

'Yeah, they all came right away, Campanella's father too. But nobody can find him. They took Zanelli home.'

Giovanni went to where everyone was milling about. Campanella's father, wearing a black suit, his jaw angular and pale, was staring at the watch gripped in his right hand. He stood tall, encircled by students and townspeople.

Everyone's eyes were fixed on the river. Not a soul was saying a word. Giovanni's legs trembled and quaked. The ripples of the black water flashed and sparkled as acetylene lamps roamed over the river, just like at fishing time.

Downstream, the Milky Way was reflected from one edge of the river to the other as if there was no water there at all but only sky. Giovanni felt that by now Campanella could be nowhere but on the very farthest edge of that river that was only sky.

But everyone still wanted to believe that from somewhere amongst the waves Campanella would appear and say, 'Boy, did I ever swim!' ... or that he would be standing on a sandbar that the people didn't even know existed, waiting for someone to find him.

All of a sudden Campanella's father spoke up emphatically.

'It's no use. It's been forty-five minutes since he fell in.'

Giovanni raced up and stood before him. I know where Campanella went. I travelled with Campanella. That's what he wanted to say, but the words just stuck somewhere in his throat.

Campanella's father, thinking that Giovanni had come to offer his sympathy, peered for some time straight into his eyes and said politely ...

'You would be Giovanni, isn't that right? Thank you for coming tonight, son.'

Giovanni bowed, unable to speak.

'Has your father come back home yet?' he asked, still gripping the watch in his fist.

'No,' replied Giovanni with a slight shake of his head.

'I wonder what could have happened? Just two days ago I had a wonderful letter from him. He should be home by about today. The boat must have been delayed, that's it. You'll come to our home tomorrow after school with everyone else, won't you, Giovanni?'

With those words Campanella's father gazed far downstream where the galaxy was part of the river itself.

Giovanni had no words for the many feelings that filled his heart. He left Campanella's father and went home to take the milk to  his mother and tell her about his father's homecoming, running as fast as his legs would take him along the river's edge towards town.

# Gauche the Cellist

It was Gauche's job to play the cello at the cinema in town. Even so, people did not think much of his playing. One could go farther and say that he was the least talented of all the musicians in the orchestra, and because of this he was given a very hard time by the conductor.

One afternoon all the musicians were sitting in a circle rehearsing the Sixth Symphony for the town's upcoming concert. The trumpets were going full blast. The violins were singing out in breezy harmony. The clarinets were tooting away, backing everyone up.

As for Gauche, he just stared at the notes with his lips pursed shut and his eyes like saucers, playing as if his life depended on it.

Without warning, the conductor clapped his hands sharply, and all the musicians stopped playing immediately. A hush fell over the orchestra.

'The cello's coming in late. To-tete tete-ti. Take if from here. Now!'

The musicians all started up again from a place just before they stopped. As for Gauche, blushing beet red and sweating bullets on his brow, he somehow managed to make his way through the part indicated by the conductor. But just as Gauche was getting into it and heaving sighs of relief, the conductor once again clapped his hands sharply.

'Cello! You're out of tune. What's gotten into you, eh? You think I've got time to go through your scales with you, do you?!'

All the other musicians, pitying Gauche, peered deliberately into their notes and tapped or fiddled with their instruments. Gauche frantically tuned his cello. There's no excusing Gauche for his playing, but the cello itself was equally to blame.

'Take it from the previous bar.  Now!'

They all started up again. Gauche twisted his lips, throwing himself into his playing. Everyone was getting through it quite well and Gauche, too, thought things were going smoothly, when the conductor scared the daylights out of them with another sharp clap of his hands. Gauche was sure he was going to get it again, but was thankful that this time the conductor had his eye on someone else. Gauche did exactly what the others had done before, namely stick his nose into his notes pretending to be mulling something over.

'So, take up from where you left off. Now!'

No sooner had they started up again when the conductor suddenly stamped his foot down.

'It won't do!' he hollered. 'You call that music? This part is the heart of the piece. It sounds like a racket the way you're playing it. My friends, we have a mere ten days left before the concert. If we professional musicians sound no better than a bunch of blacksmiths banging their anvils or a band of shop boys working in a sweets factory how can we hold up our head in public, eh?

'You, Gauche!' he continued. 'You're a real problem, you know that? Your playing totally lacks expression. Anger … joy … there's not one iota of any emotion in it. If that weren't bad enough, you're just not in sync with the others. You're always steps behind them, coming in after them as if you were tripping on your shoelaces or something. It won't do. Get your act together, will you? I feel sorry for everyone here if our shining Venus Orchestra is badly received solely on your account. So, we'll end the rehearsal here today. Have a rest and make sure you're in the pit at six on the dot.'

They all bowed, stuck cigarettes in their mouth, lit up and left the hall. As for Gauche, he carried his humble cello to a wall. He faced the wall and, pursing his lips to one side, cried like a baby. But he pulled himself together and calmly began to play the part they had been rehearsing all by himself.

Late that night, Gauche returned to his house carrying something big and black on his back. This 'house' was really a rundown watermill sitting beside a river on the outskirts of town. Gauche lived there alone. In the mornings he pruned the tomato plants in a small field that surrounded his house and picked insects off the cabbage plants, leaving sometime after noon.

He entered his house, turning on the light, and opened his big black bundle. It was really no big thing. It was his bulky, scrappy cello. He put it carefully on the floor, grabbed a glass from the shelf and gulped down some water scooped from a bucket. Then, shaking his head once, he sat in a chair and started to play that day's score with the ferocity of a tiger. Page by page he played and pondered, pondered and played, giving his all till the very end, then returning right back to the beginning, rumbling and roaring his strings.

It was long past midnight when, in the end, he couldn't even tell if it was him playing. His face was as red as a beet, his eyes bloodshot, his expression ferocious. He looked as if, at any moment, he would collapse in a heap.

It was then that someone knocked on the door behind him.

'Hauche, that you?' Gauche cried, half asleep.

But what came slipping through the opening door was a large tortoiseshell cat he had seen before. It appeared to be carrying heavy half-ripe tomatoes from Gauche's field.

'Oh, that's a load off my back. Not easy to haul these around.'

'What's the meaning of this?' asked Gauche.

'These're a present for you. Have them,' said the tortoiseshell cat.

'Who told you to bring tomatoes, eh?' yelled Gauche, in an ill humour from that day's goings-on. 'First of all, I wouldn't touch anything brought here by the likes of you! And besides, those tomatoes are from my field, you know. Outrageous picking ones that are not even ripe yet. So it's you who's been munching away on the stalks and kicking up the plants, eh? Scram, stupid cat!'

'Sir, you'll ruin your health if you get all worked up like that,' said the cat, hunching her shoulders, puckering up her mouth and grinning. 'Why don't you play Schumann's *Truе*merai instead? I'll hear it through for you.'

'Such impudence, and from a cat to boot,' said Gauche, who couldn't figure out what to do with this cat who was really getting on his nerves.

'Don't stand on ceremony just for me. Go on. You see, sir, I can't get to sleep without listening to your music.'

'Impudence, impudence, impudence!' roared Gauche, turning a fiery red and stomping his feet like the conductor did that day, but suddenly changing his mind. 'All right, I'll play.'

God knows why he locked the door, shut the windows and, picking up his cello, turned off the light. The light outside from the waning three-quarter moon shone into half of the room.

'What was that piece again?'

'*Truе*merai, by Schumann, the Rheumatic ... oh, I mean, the Romantic.'

'Okay. Is this how it goes?'

The cellist ripped his handkerchief into strips and stuffed them well into his own ears. Then he began to storm through the score of 'Hunting Tigers out in Indiah'.

The cat listened for a while with her head cocked, then suddenly blinked her eyes and, in a flash, dashed headlong for the door. She crashed right into it, but it didn't open. So, in a flurry, she let fly a splutter of sparks from her eyes and brow, as if frustrated by failure like never before in her entire life. She made a face as if about to sneeze, tickled by the sparks coming from her whiskers and nose, then, unable to stand it any longer, began to prance about. As for Gauche, he was really into his music now, playing with greater and greater zeal.

'Sir, that's enough, quite enough. I beg of you, please stop.'

'Be quiet. I'm just getting to where they catch the tiger.'

The cat, in distress, bolted up, circled about and plastered her body to the wall, leaving a trace on it that, for a while, radiated blue. In the end, she ran round and round Gauche like a little sail on a pinwheel.

'Well, then, I'll ease off for you,' he said, putting down his bow.

'Sir, something's a bit off with your playing tonight,' said the cat, as if nothing had happened up till then.

Once again, the cat's words rubbed the cellist the wrong way.

'Well, well, maybe there's something off with you!' said Gauche, nonchalantly slipping a cigarette between his lips and producing a match. 'Stick out your tongue.'

The cat thrust out her pointy tongue as if to mock Gauche.

'Oh yes, a bit on the rough side.'

Instantly the cellist struck his match on the cat's tongue and lit his cigarette. The cat was so dumbstruck that she twirled her tongue around like a pinwheel, darted toward the front door, banged her head against it, staggered, then banged it again, staggered again, all in the hope of making an escape. As for Gauche, he just stood there enjoying the scene.

'I'll let you out. Just don't ever come here again. Numbskull!'

The cellist opened the door and, faintly smiling, watched the cat dash through the reeds like a gust of wind. After that he slept soundly, without a care in the world.

The next evening, too, Gauche came home carrying the bundle that was his cello. He gulped down his water and started fiddling away. Before he knew it, it was past twelve, then well past one, then past two as well. Losing track of time, of whether he was playing or not, he was just rumbling on … when he heard a tapping noise in the attic.

'Haven't you learned your lesson, cat?'

When Gauche yelled that, a grey bird came scuffling through a hole in the ceiling. It was a cuckoo, perched on his floor.

'Now I've got a bird on my hands! What brings you here, eh?'

'I want to study music under you,' said the cuckoo composedly.

'Music?' chuckled Gauche. 'All you can sing is "cuckoo, cuckoo", isn't it?'

'You may say so, but it's frightfully difficult you know,' replied the cuckoo with an earnest air.

'Difficult? All you do is gaggle away, which any birdbrain could do.'

'You're very hard on us, you know. There's a big difference between one cuckoo's cuckoo and another cuckoo's cuckoo, if you listen carefully.'

'No difference whatsoever.'

'It's obvious that you can't tell the difference. We cuckoos can distinguish the calls of ten thousand cuckoos.'

'Suit yourself. So, if you're so smart, why did you come to see me in the first place, eh?'

'You see, I want to be able to sing my scales properly.'

'Only fish need scales!'

'Oh no, I've got to get them right before I go to foreign countries.'

'Foreign countries? Too cuckoo to even think about.'

'Sir, please teach me the scales. I'll sing along with you.'

'You're one big pain in the neck, you know that? Okay, I'll play them just three times, then, when I'm done, you get out of my sight.'

Gauche readied his cello, tuned and strummed its strings and played a scale.

'Wrong, wrong,' said the cuckoo, fluttering his wings in a flurry. 'It doesn't go like that at all.'

'Pain in the neck, you are. Okay, so you do it.'

'This is how it goes.'

The cuckoo leaned forward, posed and cuckooed.

'Ridiculous. You call that a scale? You cuckoos wouldn't know a scale from the Sixth Symphony if you heard one.'

'That's not true.'

'What do you mean not true.'

'It's just tricky when there are lots of notes in a row.'

'You mean like this?'

The cellist took up his cello again and played a series of cuckoos. The cuckoo was so overjoyed that he joined in loudly with his own cuckoos, leaning forward and singing on and on. Gauche's hands finally started hurting.

'Hey, enough is enough,' he said, putting down his bow.

The cuckoo, disappointed, continued to sing on with his eyes slanted upwards, then finally ended with a 'cuckoo-koo' and a 'cuckoo-koo-koo-koooo'.

'All right, birdie,' he said, highly strung, 'you got what you came for, now beat it.'

'I beg of you, please play one more time. Your cuckoos are not bad, they're just slightly off.'

'Off? You've got a cheek! Who's the teacher around here anyway, eh? Now, get lost!'

'Please, I beg of you, just once more. Please?'

The cuckoo bowed to Gauche over and over again.

'This is the last time, though,' said Gauche, readying his bow.

'Please string it out as long as you can,' gasped the cuckoo, bowing his head.

'This is the last straw,' said Gauche, forcing a smile.

When he started to play, the cuckoo, leaning forward, cuckooed and cuckooed with his heart and soul. At first Gauche was in absolutely no humour to play, but as he did so, he sensed that the bird's pitch was better than his. The more he played, the more keenly he felt this.

'Humph, if I keep up this ridiculous business I'll turn into a bird myself.'

Gauche instantly stopped playing. At that, the cuckoo got all dizzy, as if clunked on the head, and, with a few cuckoos and a final cuc-cuc-koo, fell silent.

'What made you stop?' he asked, looking reproachfully at Gauche. 'We cuckoos, even the more cowardly ones, cry out till blood gurgles from our throat.'

'You impudent birdbrain! How long are you going to keep up this stupid act? Just get out of here, will ya? Look, the sun's almost up.'

Gauche pointed to the window. The eastern sky was a hazy silver, and pitch black clouds were racing through it towards the north.

'Well, then, please continue on until sunrise,' said the cuckoo, bowing again. 'Once more. It won't be long.'

'Shut your beak! Trying to get away with anything you can, are you? Stupid little bird,' said Gauche, stamping his foot against the floor. 'If you don't get out, I'll pluck you clean and gobble you up for breakfast.'

The startled cuckoo suddenly flew off, making a bee line for the window. But he clunked his head hard on the glass and flopped right down.

'Look at you, birdbrain, flying right into a pane.'

Gauche went to open the window, but this window was not one to be opened easily.

While Gauche was rattling the rickety window frame, the cuckoo clunked against the panes and flopped down again. Blood trickled from the base of his beak.

'I'm opening it now, so hold your horses, will ya?'

When Gauche finally managed to open the window about two inches, the cuckoo, in a final desperate effort, with his eyes fixed on the eastern sky beyond the panes of glass, took flight as if it was the last thing he would ever do. But this time he hit a pane even harder, falling to the floor and remaining there, without budging, for some time. When Gauche reached out to grab the cuckoo to help him fly away, the cuckoo suddenly opened his eyes and sprang up, heading straight for the glass again. Gauche found himself raising up his leg and giving the window a swift kick. This shattered two or three panes with a huge crashing sound, and the window, frame and all, dropped to the ground outside.

The cuckoo flew like an arrow out of what remained of the window, and continued to fly straight away, on and on, until, in the end, he could be seen no more.

Gauche, stunned, just stared into the distance, until, after a while, plopping down in a corner of the room and falling dead asleep.

The next night, Gauche had played his cello until past midnight and, exhausted, was drinking a glass of water when someone started knocking on the door. This time, determined to throw out whoever it was just like he had the cuckoo from the night before, he sat where he was, holding his glass. The door opened a little and a tanuki cub came into his house.

'Hey, tanuki, ever heard of tanuki stew?' barked Gauche, opening the door a bit wider and stamping his foot down.

At that, the tanuki cub, a vacant look in his eyes, sat himself down on the floor.

'Tanuki stew? Haven't a clue,' he said, cocking his head as if trying to figure out what it could be.

Gauche felt like bursting into laughter, but he put a scary expression on his face instead.

'I'll tell you, then,' he said. 'Tanuki stew is made by taking a tanuki like you, mixing it up with cabbage and salt and boiling it before the likes of me wolfs it down.'

'But my dad,' said the tanuki cub curiously, 'told me to come here and learn from a really nice man like you, Mr. Gauche.'

At that, he really did burst into a laugh this time.

'Learn … that what he said, eh? Look, I'm a busy man. Besides, I'm sleepy.'

'My job's playing the small drum,' said the tanuki cub, stepping forward in a sudden burst of energy. 'He told me to beat the drum in time with the cello.'

'Drum? There's no drum around here.'

'Yes there is, here,' said the cub, producing two drumsticks from behind his back.

'And what do you propose doing with those?'

'Please play "The Merry Coachman". '

'What's "The Merry Coachman", some sort of jazz?'

'Oh, here are the notes,' said the cub, bringing a sheet of music from behind his back.

'Boy, this is some weird song,' said Gauche, laughing as he took the sheet in his hand. 'All right, then, I'll play it. You going to beat a drum, are you?'

Gauche started to play his cello, throwing glances at the tanuki cub, wondering what he was going to do. The cub started to beat time below the bridge of the cello with the two sticks. He wasn't bad at all, and Gauche got drawn into the rhythm as he played. When they had finished playing, the cub stood there for a while, cocking his head in thought.

'Mr. Gauche,' he finally said, 'it's bizarre but you fall behind when you play this second string. It makes me kind of lose my place.'

Gauche was alarmed. No matter how nimbly he played that string, the sound from it was somehow delayed.  He had noticed this the night before.

'Hmm, you might be right. Must be the cello's fault,' said Gauche, sadly.

The cub was again plunged in thought.

'Wonder what could be the matter with it,' he finally said, feeling sorry for Gauche. 'Let's give it another go, okay?'

'Fine. Here I go.'

Gauche started up again. The tanuki cub tapped out the beat like he did before, from time to time bending his neck to put an ear against the cello. By the time they had finished, the eastern sky was all hazy and bright again.

'Ah, it's dawning. Thank you very much.'

The tanuki cub slung the sheet of music and the sticks onto his back in a great rush, stuck them on with duck tape, bowed a few times and hurried away. Gauche remained where he was in a daze, for a while breathing in the wind from the window broken the day before, then, hoping to get back his strength for the next day in town, slipped under the covers and off to sleep.

The next night, too, gripping his notes and feeling very drowsy from losing himself in playing his cello right through the night until dawn, he heard knocking on his door. Even though the knocking was so faint he could barely hear it, he recognised it as knocking from the previous nights.

'Enter,' he said.

A field mouse flitted through a crack in the door with a baby mouse behind her. The baby mouse was no bigger than a pencil rubber, and Gauche found it hard to hide a smile. The field mouse looked about with googly eyes, as if wondering why Gauche was laughing at her. She came right up to him and pushed a green chestnut toward him.

'Sir, this child is very ill and could die any day,' she said, bowing formally. 'For mercy's sake, please make him well.'

'Who ever said I was a doctor?' said Gauche, a bit miffed.

The mother mouse gazed at the floor in silence.

'Sir, but you are a doctor. I mean, every day you cure everyone's illnesses, don't you?'

'What sort of nonsense is this?'

'But, sir,' she said determinedly, 'Granny Rabbit and Papa Tanuki got all better, and you even fixed up the catty horned owl, so it'd be cruel if you couldn't do something for my baby.'

'Hey now, there seems to be some mistake here,' said Gauche, taken aback. 'I've never cured any catty horned owls. And the tanuki cub just came in here last night pretending he was playing in some band or something, got it?'

Gauche smiled down at the baby mouse. Its mother burst into tears.

'Oh, this little one should have fallen ill earlier when you were playing. It would have cured him. But he got sick the moment you stopped, and if you won't play no matter how much I beg and plead, then we'll just have to accept his miserable fate.'

'Eh? You mean, my cello playing cured the catty horned owl and the rabbit?' shouted Gauche in surprise. 'What's going on here, eh?'

'That's right,' said the field mouse, rubbing her eye with her paw. 'All of the creatures around here go under your floorboards to get better whenever they're sick.'

'And that cures them?'

'It does. Their circulation improves and they feel great. Some get better right away, while others get better once they're home.'

'Oh, is that it? You telling me that the sounds from my cello sort of rumble down and your illnesses get better as if they were giving you a massage? Okay, I got it. I'll play for you.'

Gauche tightened his strings, then picked up the baby mouse between his fingers and popped him into the hole in the cello.

'I'm going with him,' the mother mouse said, frantically making a jump for the cello. 'All mothers go to the hospital with their children.'

'So you're going in too, are you,' said Gauche, trying to get the mother mouse through the hole. But only half her face went in.

'Are you all right in there?' she screamed to her baby in the cello, flapping about. 'I've always taught him that when you fall, you fall skillfully with your feet together.'

'I'm good,' answered the baby mouse from the bottom of the cello in a voice as thin as a mosquito's. 'I had a good fall.'

'He's fine,' said Gauche, looking down at the mother mouse. 'So, you don't have to wail away like that.'

Then he picked up his bow and scraped away at some rhapsody or something. The mother mouse listened with a worried expression on her face.

'That'll do. Please let him out now,' she said, controlling herself.

'Huh? Is that all you want?'

Gauche leaned the cello to one side, placing his hand against the hole. The baby mouse popped right out of the hole. Gauche put him down without saying anything. The baby mouse's eyes were shut tight and he was shivering and shaking like a leaf.

'How was that, eh? Good? How you feeling?'

The baby mouse didn't say a word, but just shivered and shook with his eyes shut tight until, in an instant, he stood up and dashed about the floor.

'Oh, he's better,' said the mother mouse, running around with her child. 'Thank you, thank you.'

Then she stood before Gauche and bowed, thanking him profusely. As for Gauche, for some reason he felt quite sorry for them.

'Hey, do you mice eat bread?' he asked.

'No thank you,' she said, staring about the room. 'I am aware that this bread of yours is made from wheat dough that is kneaded and steamed until it swells all up into something very delicious, but, having said that, we have never once visited your shelves and, besides, how could we presume to take home some of your bread after all you have done for us?'

'No, you've misunderstood. I just wanted to know if you ate bread or not. So, you do eat it. Just a second. I'll give some to your child for his sore tummy.'

Gauche laid his cello on the floor, pinched a morsel of bread off a loaf on the shelf and put it in front of them. The mother mouse, beside herself with tears and laughter, bowed to him, put the bread carefully between her teeth and left with her baby in the lead.

'All this talking to mice has really exhausted me.'

Gauche collapsed into his bed and, before he knew it, was dead to the world.

Then one night, six days later, the musicians of the Venus Orchestra, their faces flushed, left the stage in succession for the waiting room in the town hall, all carrying their instruments. They had gotten through the Sixth Symphony with flying colours. Stormy applause were still ringing out in the hall. The conductor made his way lazily amongst them with his hands in his pockets, as if he couldn't give a fig about the audience's reaction. Actually, he was bursting with delight. The musicians were all lighting up their cigarettes or replacing instruments in their cases.

Applause still rang out in the hall. Far from abating, the applause got louder and louder, until it sounded like thunder. The emcee for the evening entered with a white ribbon stuck to his chest.

'They're clamouring for an encore. Won't you give them something short?'

'No way,' said the conductor brusquely. 'After such a stupendous piece, whatever we played would be bound to be a letdown.'

'But, won't you just go out and at least have a word to them?' said the emcee to the conductor.

'Out of the question. Hey, Gauche, why don't you play something for them?'

'Me?' said Gauche, flabbergasted.

'Yes, you, you,' piped in the first violin, raising his head.

'So, out you go,' said the conductor.

They all made Gauche pick up his cello, then, opening the door, gave him a shove towards the stage. When he got to the stage, feeling embarrassed with his cello in his hands, the audience went even wilder with applause. There were even people who let out shouts. 'How much humiliation can a man take? Okay, I'll show them all. I'll play "Hunting Tigers out in Indiah". '

Gauche, now perfectly composed, stepped out into the middle of the stage. Then, just like the time the cat visited him, he played the tiger hunting piece with the ferocity and energy of an angry elephant. The audience listened intently, without making a twitter. Gauche continued to make his way through the piece, from the part where the distressed cat sparked off to the part where she incessantly rammed into the door.

When it was all over, Gauche escaped with his cello into the greenroom just like a cat, without looking at anyone. All the musicians, and the conductor too, just sat there in silence, staring straight ahead, like people who had just been through a fire.

As for Gauche, he seemed beyond caring. He walked quickly amongst them straight to a divan, plopping down into it and crossing his feet. All the musicians turned their gaze on him. They weren't laughing at him at all. In fact, they looked very serious.

'This is one pretty weird evening,' thought Gauche.

The conductor stood in front of him.

'Gauche, you were brilliant. The piece is no masterpiece, but you held our attention wonderfully. You've made great progress in a week or ten days. Ten days ago you were a babe in arms. Today you're a trooper!  You really had it in you all along, you did!'

All his colleagues came up to him, saying 'Well done.'

'You know, he can do it because he's so robust,' said the conductor standing behind the musicians. 'It would've killed an ordinary human.'

It was late that night when Gauche got back home. First he gulped down his water.

After that, he opened his window and, gazing into the distant sky where the cuckoo had appeared to fly away, he said …

'Oh, cuckoo. Please forgive me for what I did. It wasn't out of anger, I promise you that.'

# The Restaurant of Many Orders

Two young gentlemen, dressed in an utterly British military fashion with rifles sparkling on their shoulders and two dogs that resembled polar bears at their heels, were chatting to each other as they went on their way amidst the rustling leaves deep into the very heart of the mountains.

'Damn these mountains, that's what I say. No birds or animals here either. I'm just itching to blast something and I don't care what it is!'

'I'd get such a kick out of planting two or three shots smack between the yellow ribs of a deer. It'd spin round before hitting the dirt with the hugest thud!'

They were really in the heart of the mountains now, so deep that even their guide, a professional hunter, had lost his bearings and gone off somewhere.

What's more, the mountains were so scary that the two dogs resembling polar bears both became dizzy, growled for a while, frothed at the mouth and promptly died.

'Well, there goes 2,400 yen,' said one of the gentlemen, briefly rolling back his dog's eyelid.

'I'm down 2,800, you know,' said the other bitterly, his head drooping down.

The first gentleman, looking off colour and disgruntled, studied the face of the second gentleman as he spoke.

'I reckon it's time to be heading back.'

'You know, I've just been feeling rather cold and hungry, and I was thinking the very same thing.'

'Well, then, let's call it a day. Come what may, we can buy ourselves about ten yen worth of wild fowl at yesterday's inn and take that home with us.'

'Saw some rabbits there too. No one'll know the difference. Okay, let's get going back.'

However, the awful thing about it was that they didn't have the foggiest idea of which way back was.

The wind bellowed, the grass swished, the leaves rustled and the trees rumbled low.

'You know, I'm starving. My sides have been aching since way back there.'

'Me too. I don't feel like taking another step. God, what can we do? I'd give my right eye for something to eat.'

'I could eat a horse.'

That's what the two gentlemen said as they made their way through the swishing pampas grass. Then suddenly they looked back to see a magnificent European-style house behind them. A sign on the front door said …

'Hey, just what the doctor ordered. This place here is pretty civilised. Why don't we just go on in!'

'Gosh, who would've expected it in a place like this? Anyway, they're bound to be serving up something in there.'

'Of course they're serving up something. Can't you read the sign?'

'What're we waiting for, then?  If I don't get some food into this belly of mine, I'll be a goner.'

The two men stood in the entrance hall. It was a truly grand hall made of white porcelain bricks. This notice appeared in gilded lettering on the glass French doors in front of them.

> Feel Free To Enter Whoever You Are
> Please Do Make Yourselves at Home

The two men, beside themselves with joy, spoke up.

'Well, how do you like that, things are really coming our way here. We got ourselves into a pickle all day today, but we've made it now. This place is a restaurant, but they don't charge for their meals.'

'Looks that way, doesn't it. That's what they mean when they say "Please do make yourselves at home."'

The two men pushed the doors open and entered, coming right into a corridor. This was written in gilded lettering on the inside of the glass doors …

> We Particularly Welcome With Open Arms
> Plump And Young Individuals

The two men were overjoyed at being welcomed with open arms.

'See, we're being taken in with open arms.'

'Because we're both plump and young, that's why.'

They strode down the corridor to a door painted sky blue.

'This place is weird, you know.  What're all these doors doing here?'

'It's the Russian style. It's always like this in cold places and in the mountains.'

Then, as they went to open the door, they noticed some yellow writing above it.

> This Restaurant Is A Restaurant of Many Orders
> We Beg Your Indulgence

'Must be doing a roaring business! Way out here, of all places …'

'You bet. I mean, even your big Tokyo restaurants are mostly off the main streets, aren't they?'

The two men opened the door as they spoke. On the other side of it …

> You May Find There Are Many Orders
> But Please Put Up With All of Them

'What in the hell do they mean by that?' said one gentleman, scowling.

'Yeah, well, they must mean that they're apologising for the delays because they've got their hands full due to the large number of orders.'

'That must be it. I wish I could get right into one of the rooms, though.'

'And I'm dying to sit myself down at a table.'

But unfortunately there was another door there to annoy them. There was also a mirror hanging beside it and, below the mirror, a brush with a long handle. The following words were written in red lettering on the door …

> To Our Most Valued Customers
> Kindly Straighten Your Hair Here
> And Remove The Mud From Footwear

'Stands to reason. I was wrong to write them off back there at the front door as just a place in the woods.'

'They're strict on etiquette. I bet they get a lot of pretty important people here all the time.'

At this the two men combed their hair and removed the mud from their boots. And then, what do you know ... no sooner had they replaced the brush on its shelf than it became all fuzzy and blurry, then vanished ... and a wind howled into the room.

The two men clung to each other in alarm, banged the door open and entered the next room. If they didn't get back to their old selves quickly by eating some warm food, who knows what could happen. Another bizarre sign greeted them on the other side of the door ...

Be Sure To Leave Your Firearms And Bullets Here

They noticed a black stand directly to one side.

'Makes good sense. It's not proper to eat and carry a rifle at the same time.'

'Wow, they really must get a lot of pretty important people here.'

The two of them removed their rifles, undoing their belts, and put them on the stand. There was another door, a black one ...

Please Remove Your Hats, Overcoats And Boots

'What do you think, should we take them off?'

'We've got no choice. Off they go. They really must be pretty important people, I mean, the people in there.'

The two men hung their hats and overcoats on hooks, yanked off their boots and padded through the door.  Written on the other side was …

> Please Leave Here All Necktie Pins, Cufflinks
>
> Glasses, Wallets And Anything Made of Metal
>
> Particularly Items With Sharp Points

An impressive safe, painted black and with its door ajar and a key in the lock, stood directly to one side of the door.

'Oh, I reckon they're using electricity for their dishes. Metallic things are dangerous.  Pointy things are especially dangerous in that case.'

'Must be the case. So I guess you pay the bill on your way out.'

'Looks that way.'

'Must be. Sure.'

The two men took off their glasses, removed their cufflinks, put everything in the safe and locked the door. A little farther along there was another door with a glass jar in front of it.  The following words were written on the door …

> Please Cover Your Face And Limbs
>
> With Cream From The Jar

The jar definitely appeared to be full of cream made from milk.

'What do they want us to put cream on for?'

'Well, you see, it's freezing outside, right? And the room's so warm that your skin will get chapped, and they want to protect you from that. It really looks like they've got some pretty important people in there. It means that, for all we know, we might rub shoulders with aristocrats!'

They two of them rubbed cream over their faces, then over their hands and finally, taking off their socks, over their feet too. After that there was still some cream left, so they slipped some of it into their mouth while pretending to smear it on their face. Then they rushed to open the door and saw on the inside …

Did You Apply The Cream Thoroughly?
Did You Rub It Over Your Ears Too?

… and they found a small jar of cream there as well.

'Oh, yeah, I didn't do my ears. Think of how chapped the skin on them could've gotten.  The proprietors here don't leave a thing to chance, do they?'

'Yeah, they're real sticklers for details, they are. Now, I'm starving, but this place is all just one corridor after another.'

Just then they found themselves standing in front of yet another door …

The Food Will Be Ready Very Soon Now
It Won't Be Even A Bare 15 Minutes
Until Everybody's Eaten
Please Sprinkle The Perfume In The Bottle
All Over Your Heads

There was a gilded bottle of perfume in front of the door. The two men splashed perfume from it all over their head. The perfume, however, had a distinct fragrance of vinegar.

'This perfume stinks of vinegar.  What in the hell is going on here?'

'Must be some mistake. The maid caught a cold or something and put in the wrong stuff.'

They opened the door and went in. These words were written in big lettering on the back of the door …

> All of These Many Orders Have No Doubt Annoyed You
> You Have Our Sympathy
> You Have Reached The End Now
> We Only Ask That You Rub Salt From The Pot
> Thoroughly Into Your Skin

Sure enough, a splendid blue porcelain salt pot stood before them, but this time the two men stared at each other aghast, their faces swimming in cream.

'I smell a rat here, you know.'

'Yeah, something's fishy here.'

'When they say there are lots of orders, they mean they're doing the ordering on us.'

'You see, the way I figure, this European restaurant is not a place where they feed their customers European food, it's a place where they make European food out of their customers to eat them. It's uh, I ... I ... mean ... it's ... it's us who's the ...'

He was shaking and quaking so much that the words wouldn't come out.

'You mean, it's ... it's ... us who's going to be ...? Yipes!'

He too was shivering so much that he couldn't get the rest of his words out either.

'Let's get out of ...'

One of the gentlemen, shaking like a leaf, tried to push the door behind him but, wouldn't you know it, it wouldn't budge an inch. There was one more door farther along with two large keyholes in it. On the door were carvings of a silver knife and fork ...

> We Appreciate The Pains You Have Taken
> The Preparations Have Been Completed Admirably
> Now It Is Time For You To Be Consumed

That was the handwriting on the door. To cap it off, two blue eyeballs were ogling them through the keyholes.

'Yipes!' said one gentleman, trembling.

'Cripes!' said the other, shivering.

The two of them began to bawl. Then they heard whispering coming from the door.

'Oh no, they've caught on. Looks like they won't rub the salt in.'

'What do you expect, eh? The boss can't write worth beans. "All of these many orders have no doubt annoyed you … you have our sympathy" … writing like that, how stupid can you get!'

'What's the difference? He doesn't even toss us a bone, whatever we do.'

'You said it. And he'll blame us if these two guys don't come in here.'

'Let's call out to them, okay? Hey, customers. Come in now. Come on, don't be shy. The plates have been washed and the greens have been rubbed thoroughly with salt. All that remains is to arrange you tastefully among the greens on a clean white plate. Do come on in.'

'Yeah, come on. You're welcome. Maybe you don't fancy salad. In that case, we'll put the fire on now and deep fry you. Don't just stand there!'

The painful ache in the gentlemen's heart caused their faces to crumple like scraps of paper. Quivering and shivering, they stared at each other and silently sobbed.

Snickering and sniggering came from the door, along with another loud call.

'Come on in! Come on in! If you cry like that you'll just smear all that nice cream off. Yes, sir, immediately, sir. We will have them for you momentarily. Now, gentlemen, gentlemen, what are you waiting for?'

'Get yourselves in here now. The boss has already tucked in his napkin, he's got his knife poised and he's licking his chops in anticipation of his customers.'

The two gentlemen just wept and wept and wept and wept. Just then, sounds came out of the blue from behind them.

'Ruff. Ruff. Grrrr-ruff!'

The two dogs that resembled polar bears came crashing through the door and charging into the room. The eyeballs in the keyholes disappeared in a flash as the dogs circled the room for a time, snarling and growling, then, barking loudly again, suddenly threw themselves at the door.

The door crashed open and the dogs flew through it as if being swallowed up. Then the gentlemen heard a meowing, a grunting, a rumbling and finally a rustling in the pitch darkness beyond the door. The room vanished in a cloud of smoke, and the gentlemen were standing in the grass, shivering and quivering from the cold. One look and they saw their coats and boots and wallets and necktie pins hanging off branches or strewn by the roots of a tree.

The wind bellowed, the grass swished, the leaves rustled and the trees rumbled low.

The dogs returned, groaning and growling. Then there was hollering from behind.

'Gentlemen! Gentlemen!'

This suddenly brought them back to life.

'Hullo, hullo, we're over here!  Come quick!' they screamed.

The professional hunter, wearing a reed hood, approached, rustling through the grass. The two gentlemen were finally able to breathe easily. They ate the dumplings the hunter had with him, spent about ten yen on wild fowl on their way and went on home to Tokyo.

Be that as it may, neither their return to Tokyo nor long soaks in hot baths could bring those faces, crumpled like scraps of paper, back to normal again.

# The Magnolia Tree

A DAMP AND GLOOMY FOG HUNG OVER EVERYTHING.

Ryoan was making his way under the blanket of fog, tramping up and down the steep slopes of the valley.  He plodded on and on, the sole of his shoe half worn through, from peaks that reached to the heavens to the darkest deepest bottom of valleys, and once again upwards to the next towering cliff, swallowed up in fog.

The thought occurred to him that, if it was possible to swim through that fog, he would sail like the wind from one cliff straight to another. As it was, he had no choice but to trudge up the precipitous punishing surfaces of these monstrous sculptures then down again to the flatter planes below, his body burning and his breath panting as he crawled over the earth.

Black jagged boulders whistled in the freezing fog.  Though feeling desolate and totally alone, he put his heart and soul into trekking up and down.  Even the huge clump of little blackish shrubs growing in the depths of the valley looked cruel the way they absorbed all the light around them.  And yet, this did not deter Ryoan, who continued all by himself on his way from one notched peak to the next.

No sooner did the fog suddenly glow with a dim light than it slid back into half darkness. This occurred again and again. The dim whitish light would simply not give in to night.

Ryoan came to a gently sloping area where lustrous snake's beards blanketed the ground. He threw himself down, dozed off and was soon dead to the world.

'This is your world, you know. This is the world that suits you down to the ground.  But really, more than that, it's the landscape inside you, you know.'

Someone, or maybe Ryoan himself, was screaming that over and over again not far from his ear.

'That's right, that's right, that's absolutely right.  This is obviously my landscape.  It's me.  So there's not much I can do about it,' replied Ryoan, nodding off.

*'The seductive clump …*
*The training ground of spring*
*Where you learn*
*To treat all*
*Without malice'*

The voice could clearly be heard coming from somewhere. Ryoan opened his eyes. The chilling fog permeated his entire body. The fog was now so white that it hurt the eyes, and the blue slope of snake's beards glimmered faintly inside it.

Ryoan dashed down the mountain. But he caught his foot in one of the shrubs and tumbled to the ground. He stood up, a wry smile on his lips. A precipice of small trees appeared suddenly before his eyes.  He climbed up it, clinging to the branches of those spicewood trees. The spicewood trees sent a faint fragrance into the fog, and the fog afforded Ryoan something soft smooth and milky white in return. Ryoan smiled as he clawed his way up the side of the mountain.

It was then that the fog turned all gloomy, and Ryoan threw it that faint smile of his.  At that, the fog brightened up again.

Finally, he reached a plateau of withered grass.  Standing there, he felt all warm and golden, and he sensed that the faint odour of sweat was leaving his body in thin threads, surging up into the fog. A single spectacular black horse emerged, prancing out of that thought, then disappearing into the fog.

The fog, in an instant, pitched and rolled, and Ryoan caught sight of something that looked like floating amber molecules, glittering brightly.  In a flash those amber molecules were gleaming gold, then fresh green, pelting down like the rains.

Ryoan's dim shadow fell onto the withered grass.  A sliver of his fragrant odour flashed and glistened, travelling straight through the suspension of that fog and amber-green mass.  But before he knew it, the whole scene was drenched in gold again.

The fog melted away.  The sun swayed like a liquid, to and fro, in the newly polished azurite sky, and the bright wax of unmelted fog that did remain dripped down, here and there, into the valley.

'Ah, that's where I've just been, that awful sheer valley.  But what a spectacular sight this is!  And, let me see, there's that, too!'

Ryoan didn't believe his eyes.  In the countless crags of the valley, sheets of white magnolia flowers were blooming, silver in colour when struck by the sun, more like snow where not.

*'Enveloping the steeply notched*
*Cliffs on the heart …*
*Could it be young magnolia flowers?'*

This voice from somewhere could clearly be heard. Ryoan took in the scene with a heart full of light.

There was a single tall magnolia tree standing not far in the distance, with two children on either side of its trunk.

'Ah, it was those children who were singing a moment ago.  But wait … they're not just plain kids.'

Ryoan took a really good look at them.  They were like a dream in a fasting dawn, dressed in gossamer and sacred raiments, glittering in the light of the sun.  But it seems that the song had not been sung by them.  That's because one of the children had been singing in a thin voice from long before that, glaring up to the very top of the magnolia tree.

*'Santa Magnolia*
*Shining bright to the tips*
*Of your every branch'*

The child on the other side replied …

*'Silver dove soaring*
*To the heavens'*

The first child sang again …

*'Heavenly dove descending*
*From the heavens'*

Ryoan quietly continued on his way.

'This tree is Nirvana.  Where are we?'

'We don't know,' answered one of the children humbly, raising its bright eyes.

'Yes, the magnolia tree is Nirvana.'

The unwavering clear voice came to Ryoan from behind. He quickly turned around. A man just like him, dressed like the children, was standing perfectly straight alongside them.

'Was it you singing back there before?'

'Yes, me.  But it's also you. If you want to know why, it's because you can sense me.'

'Yes, I can … thank you … it's me … and it's also you. It's because, whatever is me is also in you.'

The man laughed. The two of them bowed lightly to each other for the first time.

'It's really so flat here,' said Ryoan, gazing at the beautiful golden grassy plateau behind him.

'Yes,' said the man, smiling, 'it is flat.  But the flat here is only flatness in comparison with the steepness.  It's not a real flatness.'

'That's right. It's flat because of the steep mountains I climbed to get here.'

'Look! Those steep mountains are covered in magnolia blossoms.'

'I see. Thank you.  So, then, the magnolia is Nirvana. Those petals are softer than the goat's milk of Paradise.  Its fragrance wafts exalted poetic prayer to those who have attained Enlightenment.'

'It is all goodness itself.'

'Whose goodness?' asked Ryoan, taking a last look at the magnolias on the golden plateau and the steep faces of the mountains.

'The goodness of the Enlightened.'

His shadow fell, purple and transparent, into the grass.

'Yes … and it is our goodness, too. The goodness of the Enlightened is absolute. It appears in the magnolia tree, as it does in the cold boulders of the steep cliffs. The dark dense forests of the valleys and the rivers flowing on and on and the frequent revolutions and famines and epidemics that occur where those rivers flood … all is the goodness of the Enlightened.  But here, the magnolia tree is the goodness of the Enlightened and, at the same time, our own.'

The two of them bowed again, respectfully, to each other.

# Indra's Net

IT SEEMED THEN THAT I HAD COLLAPSED, OUT OF UTTER EXHAUSTION, on a bed of green grass and wind.

In that faint of autumn wind, I exchanged bows, courteous to a fault, with my tin-coloured shadow.

Then, I stepped alone onto a dark cowberry carpet and travelled about the Tsela Plateau.

The cowberry boasted red fruit.

The white sky blanketed the entire plateau. It was a cold white, whiter than kaolin china.

The rarefied air sang in a high-pitched whirr, no doubt due to the sun making its lonely way beyond the white porcelain clouds. The sun had already sunk below the black barbed ridges in the west, creaking in the dim light of a late afternoon.

I looked around, gasping like a fish.

Wherever I looked, there wasn't even a shadow of a bird, nor was there so much as a trace of any gentle beast.

'What on earth am I visiting here in the upper reaches of the atmosphere, moving around in this air that cuts through me?'

I asked this of myself.

The cowberry was, before I knew it, gone, and the ground was covered in a sheet of dry ash-coloured moss. Red moss flowers were blossoming here and there. But all this did was to intensify the cold grief of the plateau.

Before long, the late afternoon was in twilight, the moss flowers appeared reddish black, and the colour of the sky above the ridges turned a faint and sombre yellow.

It was then that I caught sight of an all-white lake far in the distance.

'That's not water! It's natrium salt or something that's crystallised,' I said to myself. 'I mustn't lose heart by getting all content and taken in.'

Even so, I hurried over there.

The lake came closer, glittering. Before I knew it, I was gazing at pure-white quartz sand and, beyond that, a place brimming darkly with real water.

The sand squeaked. I picked up a pinch of it and examined it in the dim light of the sky. It was made up of dihexagonal pyramid grains.

'This has come from dacite or rhyolite.'

That's what I figured, whispering to myself, standing on the water's edge.

'Hey, this is supercooled water!' I whispered in my mind. 'This is the granddaddy of water in both a liquid and a solid state!'

My palm absolutely gave off a pale phosphorescence in the water.

Suddenly there was a high-pitched ring all around.

'It's the wind. It's the spears of grass. Thundering!' These were the words ringing in my head. It was pitch dark, pitch dark with a faint tinge of red.

I opened my eyes wider.

Night had fallen and the sky was as transparent as it could ever be. The water of the galaxy flowed silently over the sky's plain which was made of beautifully fired, polished steel. Little corundum pebbles shined; and every grain of sand on the banks could be counted.

The cold dark-violet plate of the sky was studded with the cleavage planes of diamonds and pointy grains of sapphire; and fragments of citrine the size of smoke bush seeds had been picked up in exquisite tweezers and inlaid into it; and all of this separately and on its own breathed in and out, trembling and quaking.

When I took another look at where my feet were, small yellow and blue flames were flickering and twinkling in the grains of sand in the sky. I suppose that supercooled lake in the Tsela Plateau was a part of the galaxy itself.

Yet, dawn seemed to come quickly on the plateau.

It was very clear that something like glassy molecules you could see right through were floating up into the air; and, above all, what looked like a fountain in the sky surrounded by nine small blue stars in the east was quickly transformed in the terribly dim light of the sky from steel to amazonite.

I saw an angel fly through space that had a dark-violet, subtle sheen.

'At last it's slipped in,' I thought, my heart jumping with delight. 'It has suddenly made its way from the Tsela Plateau of the realm of humans to that of the heavens.'

The angel soared straight ahead.

'It's covering ten kilometres in the blink of an eye!' I whispered to myself. 'But look! It isn't even budging. It's soaring ahead so far without moving, without changing place, without changing form.'

The angel's robe was as thin as smoke, and its holy necklace absorbed whispers of light from the dimly-lit plate of the sky.

'Got it,' I thought. 'The air here is rarefied almost to the point of becoming a vacuum. That's why there's no wind disturbing the folds in that delicate robe.'

The angel opened its dark blue eyes wide but didn't blink them once. It soared absolutely straight ahead with the faintest smile on its lips. Yet, it was neither moving, nor changing place or form.

'This is the place where all aspirations are purified. The number of wishes is submerged. Gravity is neutralized within itself, and a cold scent of quince floats through the air.  And so, the cord on the angel's robe neither ripples, nor does it hang straight down.'

But then the amazonite in the sky was transformed into a weird plate of purple agate, and I could no longer see the figure of the soaring angel.

'This is the Tsela Plateau after all,' I said, explaining it to myself. 'You can't count on just one single episode of blending.'

But what was strange was that the cold quince-like scent was still permeating the sky. And once again I sensed that this mysterious world in the sky was like a dream.

'There's something really puzzling here!' I thought to myself, standing there. 'This celestial space seems to be right beside my sensations. As I walk on the path here and fragments of mica gradually appear in great number, it seems to me that I am getting closer and closer to granite. It may be just a fluke, but the more often it appears this way, the truer it gets. I'm sure I'll be able to sense this celestial world on this plateau again.'

I turned my eyes from the sky to the plateau. The sand was now as pure white as can be. The blue of the lake, now more ancient-looking than verdigris, gave my heart a chill.

Suddenly I saw three heavenly children before me. They wore the thinnest robes, woven, it seemed, from frost, and transparent shoes, standing on the water's edge, peering intently into to eastern sky, as if waiting for the sun to rise. The eastern sky was already alight with whiteness. From the folds in their robes I could tell they were from Gandhara. I recognized them as being from a fresco that I had excavated at the ruins of the great Khotan Temple. I approached them quietly and greeted them in a very low voice, so as not to frighten them.

'Good morning, children of the fresco at the great Khotan Temple.'

The three of them turned toward me. Ah, the radiance of their holy necklaces and their imposing and magnificent black eyes!

I spoke again, continuing to approach them.

'Good morning, children of the fresco at the great Khotan Temple.'

'And who may you be?' asked the child on the right, looking straight at me without blinking.

'I am Aoki Akira, who excavated the great Khotan Temple from beneath the sands.'

'And what are you doing here?' said the same child, looking sternly at me straight in the eye.

'I want to worship the sun together with you.'

'The sun? It won't be long for you to wait.'

The three of them turned away from me. Their necklaces briefly shined like yellow and bitter-orange and green needles, and their robes fluttered in the colours of the rainbow.

In the fiery platinum sky, from the edge of the olive-green field beyond the lake, something that looked like it was melted, something seductive, as old as gold, crimson like that seen in a kiln, a single ray of light appeared.

The heavenly children stood perfectly erect and brought their hands together, looking towards it.

It was the sun.  It was the sun of this heavenly realm, solemnly rocking its strangely round body that was like a thing melted down, in an instant climbing properly up in the sky.  Its light now flowed in needles and bundles, and everywhere you looked you could hear a clicking and clacking.

The heavenly children jumped up and down in rapture, running over the silica sand of the pure-blue lake of True Enlightenment. Then suddenly one of the children bumped into me, and jumping back, screamed out while pointing up to the sky.

'Look, look, look at Indra's net!'

I looked up at the sky. The zenith was now azure blue, and from it to the four corners of the pale edges of the sky, Indra's spectral net vibrated radiantly as if burning, its fibres more fine than a spider's web, its construction more elaborate than that of hypha, all blending together transparently, purely, in a billion intermingled parts.

'Look, heavens, it's the drums of the wind!' said another child, bumping into me and running off in a flurry.

What can only be seen as the sun's minus counterparts, shining indigo dark and gold and green and ashen, drums seemed to fall from the sky, and, impervious to human striking, pounded out a sound with all their might; and while those countless heavenly drums called out, they seemed to be making no sound at the same time. I watched it all for so long that my eyes clouded over and all I could do was stagger about.

'Look, look at the blue peacock!' quietly said the same child who was on the right as he walked by me.

Sure enough, beyond Indra's net in the sky, on the far edge of those countless resounding heavenly drums, an enormous and strange blue peacock, fanning out its jewelled tail feathers, sang out in an ethereal voice. That peacock was most certainly present in the sky. Yet, it was not to be seen at all. It was certainly crying out. Yet its cries were not to be heard at all.

After that, there was no way that I could see the three heavenly children.

Far from it, I vaguely recalled my own figure collapsed deep into the green grass and the hollows of the wind.

# Obbel and the Elephant
*as told by a cattleman*

### THE FIRST SUNDAY

Obbel, I gotta say, is really something. He's got as many as six rice threshers set up there that are just humming away like nobody's business.

Sixteen farmers, their faces as red as beets, were there pedalling those threshers for all they're worth, thrashing the rice plants piling up in big mounds one after the other. The straw was being thrown back just as fast, making new mountains behind them. The dust from the straw and the husks hung in the air like the yellow haze of a smoky desert.

Obbel paced back and forth about that workplace with hands clasped behind his back, smoking on his big amber pipe and taking care, with squinted eyes, to keep its ash out of the straw.

The shed was built solid, as big as a schoolhouse, but even so it was still shaking from the humming that came from six of the latest threshing machines he had installed. It was shaking enough to make your stomach growl. Obbel had it all worked out, too, because he always went in there before lunch so he could wolf down a seven-inch-long steak and a pile of potatoes as big as a mop.

Anyway, I tell ya, his business was humming along like nobody's business.

So then, for some reason or other, I mean, that white elephant just came along. We're talkin' here about a real white elephant, you know. It ain't no elephant just painted white. What was it doin' there, you ask?

Well, seein' as it's an elephant, I reckon all we can say is that it kinda wandered out of the woods one day and landed there.

When the elephant slowly stuck his head through the front door of the shed, the farmers nearly jumped outta their skin. Why did they nearly jump outta their skin? I'm tellin' ya, it's because they had no way of knowin' what the thing was gonna do, that's why! They didn't want to have anythin' to do with the thing, so each an' every one of them just put their nose to the grindstone, so to speak, and got on with their threshing.

Anyway, Obbel was standing behind the line of threshers just then with his hands in his pockets, giving the elephant a good sharp look over. Then he simply continued to pace back and forth and gaze at the floor as if nothing had happened.

Well, if that white elephant didn't put one foot down on the shed floor. This caused the farmers to jump even farther out of their skin. Even so, they just kept on threshing and threshing, without so much as glancing up at the elephant.  After all, everyone knows, you don't wanna mess with an elephant, now do ya.

Obbel, taking his hands out of his pockets in the dim back part of the shed, gave the elephant another look, then resumed his pacing with his hands clasped behind his head, deliberately yawning a huge yawn as if he was bored stiff. But the elephant now just thrust both front feet into the shed, trying to get in.  The farmers jumped even further out of their skin than before, and even Obbel was a bit startled, suddenly blowing a puff of smoke out of his big amber pipe. Nonetheless, he kept on walking about, as if not fazed one bit.

Now the elephant just barged right in nonchalant-like and started to walk in front of the machines as if he had done it all his life.

Now, because the machines were humming away at full blast, the husks shot out like an evening hail, slapping the elephant in the face. The elephant squinted his little eyes. He was clearly annoyed, but, if you looked closely, you could see that he was definitely smiling a little smile all the same.

Obbel finally decided to walk to the front of the threshing machines and have a word with the elephant. But just then the elephant spoke up in a beautiful little voice, as soft and lovely as a nightingale's …

'Ah I can't take it. The sand just keeps smacking my teeth.'

Sure enough, the husks were smacking and slapping against his teeth like there was no tomorrow and hitting his pure white head and neck to boot.

Now, this was Obbel's cue to take things into his own hands. He switched his pipe from his left hand to his right, plucked up his courage and said …

'Well, whadda ya say? You havin' a nice time here?'

'Yes, very nice time,' replied the elephant with smiling eyes, leaning his body to one side

'So how about stickin' around here, eh?'

The farmers, taken totally aback, held their breath and stared at the elephant. Obbel's blurting this out sent shivers and shakes down their spine.

But the elephant just answered nonchalantly …

'It's fine with me to stick around.'

'Good, then it's settled. Yep, it's settled once and for all.'

Obbel was so overjoyed that his face turned a fiery red and wrinkles appeared all over it.

Well, so how's that? That's how the elephant became Obbel's property. An' you'll see soon enough what's in store. Will Obbel put the elephant to work? Will he sell him off to a circus? Whatever he does, he's bound to clean up.


## THE SECOND SUNDAY


Obbel, I gotta say, is really something. And, I gotta say that the elephant he so cleverly took possession of a little while ago in the threshing shed is actually really something, too. He can produce up to twenty horsepower. Above all, his appearance was all white and his tusks were made entirely of pure ivory. His skin, too, was all made of superb, solid elephant hide. And how he could work! But when all is said and done, it was his master who should get the credit for getting so much out of him.

'Hey, how'd you like to have a watch, eh?' said Obbel, scowling with his amber pipe between his teeth and standing in front of the elephant's long shed.

'I don't need one, thank you,' replied the elephant, smiling.

'Here's one anyway. A watch's a good thing,' said Obbel, hanging a huge tin watch around the elephant's neck.

'Pretty nice, I like it,' said the elephant.

'Now you need some chains.'

Obbel picked up some chains weighing a hundred kilos and attached them to the elephant's front leg.

'Pretty nice chains, I like them,' said the elephant, walking around on three legs.

'Now how about a shoe, eh?'

'I don't wear shoes, thank you.'

'Well, slip into this anyway. Shoes are good,' said Obbel, scowling and slipping the elephant's back heel into a big papier-mâché shoe.

'Pretty nice shoe, I like it,' said the elephant.

'Now the shoe needs a decoration.'

Obbel rushed to clamp a copper weight, weighing four hundred kilos, over the shoe.

'Hmm, pretty nice decoration, I like it,' said the elephant contentedly, trying to walk around on two legs.

The next day, the huge watch and the worthless paper shoe fell to pieces, and the elephant walked about fully content in just his chains and his copper weight.

'Awfully sorry,' scowled Obbel with both hands behind his back, 'but taxes are killing me, so just go to the river and bring back some water, will ya?'

'Ah, I'm happy to bring back water. I'll bring back as many bucketsful as you want.'

The elephant's eyes smiled as he brought back about fifty bucketsful of water that afternoon, spraying them all over the vegetables in the field.

The elephant stayed in his shed in the evening, eating ten bundles of straw.

'Ah, hard work is such a delight,' he said, gazing up at the crescent moon in the western sky.  'I feel like a new elephant.'

The next day, Obbel came to the elephant again, this time with his hands in his pockets and a red tasselled hat on his head.

'Really sorry,' he said, 'but the taxes now are murderous. So just go to the forest and bring me back some firewood, will ya?'

'Ah, I'm happy to bring back firewood,' smiled the elephant. 'It's such a beautiful day today. There's nothing more I love than to go to the forest.'

A bit startled, Obbel almost dropped his pipe right out of his hands, and the elephant, looking as happy as a lark, just started to slowly walk away. This set Obbel's heart at ease, and he grabbed his pipe in his teeth once more, gave out a feeble cough and went over to the farmers to see how they were working.

That whole afternoon the elephant hauled nine hundred bundles of firewood from the forest, his eyes smiling with joy all along.

That evening, in his shed, the elephant ate eight bundles of straw.

'Ah, I feel so refreshed,' he said to himself, looking up at the four-day-old moon. 'Santa Maria.'

Then the next day …

'Really sorry, but taxes have rocketed up fivefold.  Just go to the smithy's and blow on the coals, will ya?'

Ah, I'm happy to blow on the coals. If I put my heart into it, well, I tell you, I can knock over big boulders with my breath.'

Obbel was startled again to hear this, but he composed himself and smiled a big smile.

The elephant plodded down to the smithy's, flopped down on his knees and blew on the coals like bellows.

That evening in the elephant shed, the elephant ate seven bundles of straw and looked at the five-day-old moon and said, 'Ah, I'm so tired … and so happy. Santa Maria.'

So whadda ya know? From the next day, the elephant worked himself from the early morning. And the day before he had eaten only five bundles of straw. It's amazing how he can be so strong on only five bundles of straw.

The elephant's a real money-saver. But you gotta hand it to Obbel. He's the clever one, the brilliant one. Yeah, that Obbel's really something.


## THE FIFTH SUNDAY


WHAT? OBBEL? OH YEAH. WELL, THIS OBBEL … THAT'S WHAT I'M trying to tell ya! … so this Obbel … was no more. Just calm yourself and listen, will ya! The elephant I was tellin' you about, he was treated pretty bad by Obbel. Obbel just got harsher and harsher, and the elephant couldn't smile anymore despite himself. At times he peered down on Obbel with the red eyes of a dragon.

One evening in the elephant shed, the elephant ate three bundles of straw as he gazed up at the ten-day-old moon.

'I'm in such pain … Santa Maria,' is what he said.

Hearing this only made Obbel even more cruel.

So, one evening in the elephant shed, the elephant, unable to eat any straw at all, shaking and quaking as he sat on the bare ground and looking up to the eleven-day-old moon, said …

'This means goodbye, Santa Maria.'

'What? What's that you said? Goodbye?' said the Moon to the elephant out of the blue.

'Yes, it's goodbye. Santa Maria.'

'What's wrong with you? A big lug like you, where's your backbone, your spirit? Get yourself up and write a letter to your mates.'

That's what the Moon said, beaming down on him.

'But I don't have any brush or any paper,' sobbed the elephant, barely able to eke out his sweet little voice.

'Heavens above, look here,' came the cute voice of a child right in front of him.

And when the elephant raised his head to take a look, he saw a boy in a red robe offering him paper and ink. The elephant lost no time in writing his letter.

'I'm being treated pretty awful. Everyone please come over and save me.'

The child immediately set out for the woods with the letter in hand.

It was just about lunchtime when the child, in his red robe, arrived at the mountain. The elephants, who were playing go and games in the shadows of the sala trees, put their heads together and read the letter.

'I'm being treated pretty awful. Everyone please come over and save me.'

The elephants stood up all at once and roared like they had never roared before.

'Let's get Obbel!' shouted the head elephant over the din.

And they all called out in unison, 'Oh, let's get going. Grrra-gaaaaah! Grrra-gaaah!'

So … all the elephants went roaring through the woods like a storm … Grra-gaah! Grrra-gaaah! … flying on towards the fields. They had thrown all sense to the winds. Little trees and shrubs were uprooted; the groves and thickets, decimated. Gaaah … gaaah, gahaaa … gaaah! They shot into the fields like fireworks. And then … whadda ya think … they positively exploded like a volcano when they at last reached the edge of the misty blue field and caught sight of the yellow roof of Obbel's mansion.

Grrra-gaaah … Grra-gaaah!  It was precisely 1:30, and Obbel was just taking his afternoon nap on his leather bed, dreaming of crows.

Obbel's farm workers came a few steps out the front gate to see what was causing the racket, and, shading their eyes, saw what looked like a whole forest of elephants barrelling toward them, faster than a train.

'Master! It's the elephants!' they cried for dear life, running into the house as pale as ghosts. 'They're rushing toward us. Master, it's the elephants!'

But, you know, Obbel wasn't born yesterday. He realised what he had to do the moment his eyes blinked open.

'Hey, is that elephant in the shed?  Is he? Well, is he? I'm asking you, is he?  Good. Shut the door.  I said, shut the damn door! Shut the door to the shed, will ya? Yeah, go on. Now, get a big log over here and shut him up inside.  Dammit, just do as I say, will ya! Fasten the log there.  You good-for-nothings, why, you're slowin' down deliberately! That's good, now bring me five or six more logs. Yeah, that should do the trick. That'll fix it up. Don't panic!  Hey, everybody, now the gate. Shut the gate up! Bolt it up good. Get that bolt in.  Get it in!  That's right.  Hey, everybody, whadda ya worrying about, eh? Pull yourselves together, will ya?'

Obbel was now ready for the elephants, and he cheered up the farmers with his clear bugle-like voice.

But … you see, the farmers were scared to death. The last thing they wanted was to get mixed up in this by a man like Obbel. They all wound towels and handkerchiefs and dirty white cloths around their arms.  It was a sign of surrender.

Obbel ran about the place, now all worked up. Even his dog got worked up and, barking as if his tail was on fire, dashed about the mansion from one room to the other.

Before anyone knew it, the ground began to wobble and shake, and blotches of darkness appeared all around. The elephants had surrounded the mansion. 'Grrra-gaah … grrra-gaah.' And amidst that spine-tingling uproar, these words, in a gentle voice, wafted into the shed …

'We're going to save you now so don't get alarmed.'

Then came a voice from inside the elephant's shed …

'Thank you. It's so good of you to come. I'm really really happy.'

Well, at this point the elephants were roaring even louder, 'Grrra-gaaah … Grrra-gaaaah.' They must have been racing around the walls of the mansion, because you could catch glimpses of their angry trunks waving in the air. But those walls were made of concrete, with iron rods inside them, so not even an elephant could smash them down so easily.

Obbel stood inside the walls, hollering all by himself. The farmers just went around in circles in a dizzy daze. Before long, elephants were using the body of other elephants to stand on, getting high enough to scale the walls. Gradually they were poking their head over the walls. Obbel's dog fainted when he looked up at their huge grey wrinkly faces.

Well, Obbel started shooting. With his six-shooter, you know.

Bang! Graaa-gaaah. Bang! Graaa-gaaaah. Bang! Graaah-gaaah. But, you know, the bullets didn't sink in. They just bounced right off the elephants' tusks.

'Tsk-tsk, what a pain in the neck,' said one elephant. 'He keeps smacking us in the face.'

Obbel, reloading, seemed to recall having heard similar words somewhere, sometime. Before long, one elephant leg came over the top of the wall … and then, another leg. Then, five elephants thudded onto the ground all at once.

Obbel was crushed to smithereens with his ammunition case in his fist. The gate was soon opened and all the elephants poured in, one after the other. 'Graaah-gaaah! Graaah-gaaah!'

'Where's the jail?!'

All the elephants rushed to the shed. The logs bolting the door were no match for the elephants. They were smashed to bits like matchsticks. The white elephant emerged from the shed only a skinny shadow of his former self.

'Oh, thank goodness. You've lost so much weight.'

They all quietly approached him and removed his chains and copper weight.

'Ah, thank you so much. You really saved me in the nick of time,' said the white elephant with a sorrowful smile.

..... Hey, you, I told you not to go into the river!

# The Life of Budory Goosko

## THE FOREST

BUDORY GOOSKO WAS BORN IN THE HUGE FORESTS OF IHATOV. HIS father, Nadory Goosko, was a renowned woodcutter who could cut down the tallest tree without a fuss, as if lulling a baby to sleep.

Budory had a younger sister called Neri. They played in the woods every day. They went far into the woods but never so far that they couldn't hear the rasp of their father's saw as he cut down his trees. The two of them picked raspberries there, rinsing them in a spring, and took turns imitating the cry of the turtledove, gazing all the while up at the sky. At these times, the birds sleepily returned their calls in one soft cry after another.

While their mother sowed the little field in front of their house with barley, the two of them spread a straw mat on the ground, sat down on it and simmered the leaves of orchids in a tin can. Before they knew it, all kinds of birds were flapping by over the crackly hair of their head, as if greeting them hello.

When it came time for Budory to go to school, the forest turned into a frightfully lonely place in the middle of the day. But then, later in the afternoon, Budory and Neri would go all around the forest writing the names of the trees on their trunks in red clay or half-burnt pieces of old charcoal, singing at the top of their voice.

They wrote, too, on a birch tree where hop vines growing from both sides of the path formed a trellis …

To All Cuckoos   Keep Out!

And so, Budory turned ten and Neri, seven.  But, for some reason or other, the sun that year became strangely pale from springtime, and the pure white flowers of the magnolia trees just didn't blossom with the thawing of the snow, and even May saw days when sheets of sleety rain fell, and when July came it didn't bring so much as a day of heat, and the barley that was sown the year before had all white ears without grain and the flowers of most of the fruit trees just bloomed and fell straight to the ground.

Finally, autumn arrived, but the chestnuts, too, were simply shells, and the oryza that they all ate every day, so vital to them, was all husk and no grain.  There had never been a worse time for the fields.

Budory's father and mother spent a lot of time gathering firewood from the fields, and, with the winter they carried big logs to town on a sledge, but they lost heart every time, bringing back only meagre amounts of flour to eat.  Even so, they managed to get through the winter, and when spring came, they sowed the seeds that they had stored so carefully.  But that year proved to be a repeat of the year before, and the autumn brought with it a real famine.  Not a single child could be found in school.  Budory's father and mother both stopped doing any work, and there were times when, after what looked like grave deliberations, they took turns going to town, sometimes bringing back a few handfuls of millet and other times returning empty handed and at a total loss. The Gooskos passed the winter eating things like beechnuts, arrowroot, bracken stalks and the soft bark of trees.

The following spring saw both parents come down with some kind of horrible disease.

One day, Budory's father just sat there with his head gripped in his hands, plunged deep into thought.

'I'm just going to make a visit to the woods,' he said, rising abruptly.

He hobbled out of the house and did not return, though the day had turned to pitch-black night. Budory and Neri both asked their mother what happened to their father, but all their mother did was stare in silence into their face.

On the evening of the next day, when the forest was enveloped in darkness, Budory and Neri's mother bolted up without warning, fed a heap of woodchips to the hearth, lighting up the entire house, told the two of them that she was going out to look for their father and that they should little by little eat the flour and things in the cupboard, and, like their father, staggered out of the house.  Budory and Neri both cried and followed her, but she turned back to them and said in a scolding voice …

'What disobedient children you are!'

She then walked briskly, tripping as she went, until she disappeared into the woods. Budory and Neri just paced back and forth and round and round, crying all the while. Finally, when they could stand it no longer, they, too, entered the forest, and, wandering and circling about by the hop plant trellis and the spring, they called out to their mother throughout the night. The stars twinkled amongst the trees as if trying to tell them something, and the birds shot through the darkness as if alarmed … but no human voice was heard wherever they went.  Finally, Budory and Neri returned to their house in a daze of exhaustion and were soon lost to sleep, dead to the world.

It was past noon the next day when Budory awoke.

He remembered what his mother had said about the food in the cupboard and, opening it, found a big bag with buckwheat flour and lots of beechnuts in it. Budory shook Neri awake, and they both moistened up some flour and lit a fire in the hearth just like when their parents were there.

After twenty days' time had slipped by, they heard someone at the door say, 'Hello, anyone there?'  Budory leapt to his feet, thinking that his father had come back, but standing outside the door was a man with a big basket on his back and a cutting look in his eye. The man produced a round rice cake from his basket.

'I'm here to help with the famine in these parts,' he said, tossing them the rice cake. 'Dig into this, kids.'

Budory and Neri were staggered.

'Go on, eat.  Eat it!' said the man.

Budory and Neri, unsure at first, took a few bites.

'You're good kids,' said the man, peering into their eyes. 'But it's not goin' to do you any good just bein' good kids.  You should come along with me.  But you, boy, are strong an' I can't take the two of you.  But hey, little girl, there's nothin' for you to eat if you stay on here.  Come with me to town, eh? I'll give you bread every day.'

At that, the man lifted Neri straight up off the ground, shoved her right into the basket on his back, barked out, 'Oh, goody goody, oh, goody goody,' roared with laughter and flew out the door like the wind.  Once outside, Neri began to weep and wail, as Budory dashed after them, crying and screaming, 'Robber! Thief!' But the man had already passed along the edge of the forest and was flying through the distant meadow. All Budory could hear was the faint weeping and wailing of his sister Neri.

Budory followed them as far as the edge of the forest, sobbing and shouting, but soon he was completely out of breath and collapsed in a heap on the ground.


## THE SILKWORM FACTORY

BUDORY ABRUPTLY OPENED HIS EYES AND HEARD A FLAT, LOW-pitched voice coming from right over his head.

'So, you finally managed to wake up. Plannin' on starvin' to death, are ya? Well, get up and give me a hand.'

A man with a brown mushroom of a cap on his head and an overcoat hugging his shirt was dangling something made of wire in front of him.

'Is the famine over?' asked Budory. 'What am I supposed to give you a hand with?'

'Net throwing.'

'Are you going to throw nets over here?'

'Yep, sure am.'

'What are you going to do with them after that?'

'Breed silkworms, that's what.'

Two men on ladders seemed to be hard at work casting nets over the chestnut trees, adjusting them here and there. Yet the nets were so fine that Budory couldn't see their threads.

'Is that how you raise silkworms?'

'Yep, sure is. You're a persistent little kid, you know that? Listen here, you're starting this off on the wrong foot, little man. It takes more than luck to get something like this off the ground. Why would I go puttin' up a silkworm factory in a place where ya couldn't produce thread? We're all set up to do it here. There's actually a lot of folks like me makin' ends meet out here doin' this very thing.'

'Oh, well then …' Budory finally eked out in a scratchy voice.

'An' besides, seein' as I've bought up all the woodland here, you can work here if you want or, if not, you can just get lost and go off somewhere else. I mean, it's not as if you're goin' to find anything more to eat anywhere else, is it.'

'If that's the case, I'll help out,' said Budory, barely managing to hold back his tears. 'But, why are you casting nets over the trees?'

'Sure, look, I'll tell you all about it. See this?' With both his hands the man pulled on the wires of what looked like a cage. 'See? If you pull like this, you get yourself a ladder.'

The man strode over to the chestnut tree on his right and hooked the wire ladder onto a low branch.

'Now, try and take this net up to the top. Go on, climb up now.'

The man handed Budory a funny-looking ball-like object. There was nothing for Budory to do but take it and, holding fast to the ladder, he started to climb up. The rungs of the wire ladder were thin and they virtually bit into his hands and feet.

'Keep climbin'! Higher, higher! Now, throw that ball I gave you. Throw it right over the chestnut tree. Throw it high up into the sky. What's the matter with you, shakin' like a leaf? Good-for-nothin' kid!

Throw it. Throw the damn thing, will ya!'

Budory had no choice but to fling the ball-like object with all his might up into the blue sky. But just then the sun shone black in his eyes and he fell topsy-turvy out of the tree towards the ground. The man caught him, lifted him away from the ladder and absolutely flipped his lid.

'You're really good for nothin', aren't ya! What a little namby-pamby you are! If I hadn't caught you just now, you would've split your noggin right open. You owe me your life, little man, and I won't tolerate your insolence from now on. Now, get over to that tree and get yourself up it and I'll give you somethin' to eat in a bit.'

The man handed Budory another ball. Budory carried the ladder to the next tree and flung the ball over its branches.

'Thataboy, I think you've got the hang of it. Now, I've got a lot of balls where that one came from, so stay on the ball. Any one of these chestnut trees will do.'

The man took some ten balls from his pockets, gave them to Budory and marched off. But, casting just three of them made Budory short of breath and completely worn out, and he hobbled over to the house that was his home. But now, to his utter surprise, the house had a chimney made of red earthenware pipes sticking out of its roof, and over the front door a sign that read …

## THE IHATOV SILKWORM FACTORY

The man from before came out of the house smoking a pipe.

'Well, kid, I've got somethin' for you to eat here. Fill your belly and then get on the job again while it's still light.'

'I won't do it. I'm going home.'

'Home? You mean this place? This place isn't your home anymore, kid. It's my factory. The house and all the woodland here, I bought it an' it's all mine now.'

Budory was so desperate that he took the steamed bun the man was holding out and, without saying a word, marched over to a tree to cast another ten balls of net over its branches.

That night, Budory curled up into a little ball and fell asleep in the corner of what used to be his home but was now a silkworm factory.

The factory owner sat by the fire till late, drinking and talking with a few men that Budory didn't recognise. At the crack of dawn, Budory went into the woods and worked as he had the day before.

When about a month had gone by and all the chestnut trees in the forest were covered in nets, the factory owner had his men hang five or six rough planks of wood in the branches of every tree. Each plank was covered in what looked like grains of millet. Before long, the trees were sprouting leaves and the whole forest had turned an ashen blue. After a while, countless little pale-white worms were crawling off the boards and up onto the branches of the trees, leaving trails of thread behind them.

Budory and the other workers were now put to work gathering firewood every day and piling it up at the sides of the house. Pale white strings of flowers were blossoming throughout the branches of the chestnut trees, and the worms that had crawled in the branches blended in perfectly with them. After that, all the leaves on all the chestnut trees were eaten away until not even a trace of them was left.

Before long the worms were spinning large yellow cocoons throughout the mesh of the nets.

That was when the silkworm factory owner went positively berserk, hollering at Budory and the others to rush about and collect cocoons into baskets. He had all the cocoons put into cauldrons and boiled up furiously, after which the gathered thread was spun on three spinning wheels that rattled away day and night. When half the little house was full of yellow spun thread, huge white moths began to flip and flap out of the cocoons that had been left outside, flitting into the air. The factory owner, his face lit up like a demon's, now began to gather up the thread himself, and he brought four more men from the fields to join him in the work. The number of moths leaving their cocoons had grown with the days, and, in the end, it was as if snow itself was fluttering throughout the forest. Then, one day, several horse-drawn carts arrived and were loaded up with the entire store of thread before starting back towards town, followed by the workers. When the very last cart was about to leave, the silkworm factory owner turned to Budory.

'Hey, I've left enough food in the house to last you till spring. You stay here and guard the forest and the factory, you hear?'

And having said that, he followed the last cart away with a weird smirk on his face.

Budory was left alone in a daze. The inside of the house was a filthy mess, as if ravaged by a storm, and the woods themselves had been laid waste to, as if a wildfire had swept right through it. When, the next day, Budory started to clean up the house and the area around it, he came across an old cardboard box where the silkworm factory owner had often sat. There were some ten books crammed into the box. He opened the books and saw many pictures of silkworms and drawings of machines. There were also books that went above his head and those that contained pictures of various trees and plants with their names written under them.

Budory spent that winter diligently copying down the words and the drawings that were in the books.

When spring came, the factory owner appeared again, this time most impeccably dressed, bringing with him a number of new hands. From the next day, they all began to work exactly as they had the year before.

All the nets were cast over the trees and the yellow boards hung from the branches. The worms crawled off the boards up onto the branches. Budory and the others were set to work gathering firewood. One morning, when they were piling up the firewood, the earth began to shudder and quake. Then, far in the distance, a tremendous boom was heard.

After a while the day turned bizarrely dark, a fine ash came fluttering down, and a pure white sheet blanketed the forest. Budory and the others crouched down in shock under the trees, and the factory owner scurried over in a huff.

'Hey, all of you, it's over. It's an eruption. The thing has started to erupt. The silkworms have all been covered in ash and are dead. Everyone pull out. Hey, Budory, you can stick around if you want, but there won't be any food left for you this time. Besides, it's dangerous to stay on. You're better off getting yourself to the fields and working there, do you hear?'

No sooner had he said that than he was scurrying away and gone. Budory went to the factory to have a look there, but the place was deserted. So, downhearted and dejected, he headed for the fields, stepping into the footsteps that had been left by the others in the white ash.

## THE MARSH PADDIES

BUDORY CONTINUED TO WALK FOR HALF A DAY THROUGH THE ASH-covered woods towards town. Every time a wind blew, ash fluttered down from the trees in a blizzard of smoke. The closer he got to the paddies, the thinner and sparser the cover of ash became, until once again the trees looked green and footsteps vanished in the sloshy road.

When he finally made his way out of the woods, Budory found himself gazing ahead in astonishment. Before his eyes, all the way to the clouds in the distance white as snow, paddies lay before him like so many beautifully pink, green and grey cards. As he approached them, he saw that the pink came from a low blanket of flowers and that honeybees were busy going from one to another, that the green was from densely growing grasses on which little ears had formed, and that the grey came off the shallow mud of the marsh. All of these had been marked off by low narrow embankments, and people were using horses to dig up and plough the paddies.

Budory walked amongst the paddies for a time. Two men were having what sounded like a fierce argument in the middle of the road. The man on the right, sporting a red beard, said to the other man, who was old and tall and wearing a white rush hat …

'I'm a man who bets and run risks in whatever I do.'

The other man then said …

'When I said give it up, I meant it! You can pile on as much manure as you like, but all you're goin' to get is straw without a single grain.'

'Humph, the way I estimate it, it's going to be three times hotter this summer than up to now, take my word for it.  I'm going to take in three years' worth of grain in one year.'

'Give it up while you're ahead, I say. Forget it.'

'Humph, there's no way in the world I'd do that. I've already composted heaps of flowers and beans and enough chicken manure for a 100,000 square metres. We don't have all day here and I need all the help I can get. That's why I've come to you.'

Budory, in spite of himself, went up to the men and bowed.

'Well, then, how about using me?' he said.

At that the two men, looking most startled, put their hands to their chin and stared at Budory.  The man with the red beard suddenly burst out laughing.

'Sure, sure. You can hold the horse's bit.  Follow me right now. So, it's put up or shut up. Just you watch me till the autumn. Well, let's go. All I wanted was a little help when I needed it,' said the man with the red beard now to Budory, now to the other man, as he walked away from them both.

'You'll be cryin' into your soup for not listenin' to what an old man has to say to ya,' muttered the other man as he watched the man with the red beard walk away, followed by Budory.

Each day Budory used a horse to turn the muddy soil. Each day saw the pink and green gradually squashed down into a bog. From time to time the horse kicked up muddy water that splashed into everyone's face. When one paddy was done, he took the horse into the next one. Each day was very long, and, in the end, he didn't know if he was standing or walking, and the mud just looked to him like squishy candy or watery soup. The wind barely stopped howling, forming ripples like fish scales on the muddy water nearby and turning the water in the distance the colour of tin. Bittersweet clouds puffed through the sky every day as slow as they could, and Budory looked up at them with an envious eye.

Some twenty days passed like that until all of the paddies were, at last, soft mud. The next morning, the owner of the fields, all worked up, joined all of the people who had gathered from here, there and everywhere, to plant oryza seedlings, like little green lances, in every bit of paddy mud. That took some ten days, and when it was done, he took Budory and the others to work at the houses of people who had helped out in the paddies. And when that work was finished, he returned to his own paddies and weeded and weeded and weeded some more. The owner's oryza plants turned black as they grew, while the neighbouring paddies were a fuzzy light green, making it easy to see the border between the two from far away. After seven days of weeding, they all went away again to help others in their work.

But, one morning, when the owner was taking Budory around his paddies, he suddenly stood bolt upright and screamed, 'Ah!' Even his lips had turned pale blue as he stood erect, gazing vacantly over his paddies.

'It's definitely a disease,' he finally said.

'Do you have a headache,' asked Budory.

'Not me, the oryza! That!'

The owner pointed to the stalks of the oryza in front of them. Budory crouched down to get a better look, seeing that it was true. All of the leaves were speckled with red dots the likes of which he had never seen before. The owner plodded with a heavy heart once around his paddies, then started off for home. Budory followed. He was terribly worried about him. At home, the owner wet a cloth, wrung it out, put it on his head and fell asleep right there on the wooden floor.  It was then that his wife came running in from outside.

'Is it true that the oryza's diseased?'

'Yeah, it's all finished.'

'Isn't there anything you can do?'

'Don't think so.  It's just like what happened five years ago.'

'That's why I told you to give up being a speculator, didn't I? Grandpa did his best to try to stop you, too.'

She looked completely rattled and burst into tears.  At that, her husband abruptly sat up.

'Got it,' he said, suddenly in good spirits.  'Am I not one of the greatest farmers these fields of Ihatov have ever seen … am I going to let a little thing like this defeat me?  Got it!  Next year I'm going to beat this thing.  Budory, you've not stayed over a single night since you first came to my home, have you.  Well, you sleep as long as you like, five days, ten days, however many days.  After that, you're going to see the amazing tricks I can conjure up in those marsh paddies.  But because of what happened, we'll all be eating only buckwheat this winter.  You like buckwheat, I'm sure.'

Having said that, the owner of the paddies hurriedly donned his hat and left.

Budory did as the owner said and went to the stables to sleep.  But the marsh paddies were weighing on his mind, and he made his way over there with leaden feet.  The owner, too, had gone there.  He was standing all alone on an embankment with his arms folded over his chest.  The paddies were full of water, the oryza stalks had barely given off leaves, and petrol was gleaming off the surface of the water.

'I'm now in the process of choking off this disease.'

'Will the petrol kill off what's causing the disease?' asked Budory.

'I've doused the place in petrol, and even a human would die from that,' said the owner, taking a deep breath and shrugging a shoulder.

Just then the owner of the neighbouring paddies down from his approached.

'What are you doin' puttin' petrol in the water?' he yelled, stiffening his shoulders and out of breath. 'It's all run down my way.'

'What do you mean what am I doin'?' answered the owner, cool as a cucumber. 'When oryza gets diseased, you put petrol in the water.'

'Yeah, you do that and it all runs down to me.'

'Well, what do you expect it to do? Water flows down, so naturally the petrol is goin' to flow with it.'

'So, if that's naturally what's goin' to happen, why didn't you block up the place where it flows through, eh?'

'You wanna know why I didn't block off the place where the water flows down your way?  It's because that part of the paddy isn't mine so I can't go blockin' it off, that's why!'

The other man was so furious he couldn't speak, so instead, he all of a sudden splashed right into the water of one of his paddies and began to block off the opening with handfuls of mud.

'He's a tough nut,' said the owner, grinning. 'If I blocked off the opening on my side, he'd still blow his stack and blame me, so I've got him to do it on his side.  All he has to do is block it off in one place there and my paddies will fill up with water to the tops of the plants in a single night.  Now, let's go.'

The owner started off at a brisk pace towards home.

The next morning, Budory went back to the marsh paddies with the owner, who picked a single leaf from the water and examined it thoroughly, pulling a long face.  The same thing happened the day after that, too.  And the day after that.  And the day after that.  On the morning after that, the owner finally said determinedly …

'So, Budory, it's high time we started sowing buckwheat.  Go on over there and break down that barrier to the other paddies.'

Budory did what the owner said and broke down the barrier. Water with petrol in it flowed into the neighbouring paddies with a frightening force. They were sure that the owner of those paddies would blow his stack again, and, sure enough, at just about noon, he did come back, this time wielding an enormous sickle.

'What in the hell do you think you're doin', releasing petrol into my paddies?!'

'What's wrong with a bit of petrol once in a while?' said the owner in his usual calm low voice.

'It'll kill off all of my oryza.'

'Kill it off or not, just have a look at the oryza in my paddies, will ya? This is the fourth day since I covered the plants with petrol. And, you can see for yourself what the result is. The ones with the red spots are the sick ones, the vigourous ones are that way because of the petrol. The petrol has only barely flowed up to the stalks in your paddy. Might do 'em the world of good, for all I know.'

'You mean, the petrol's a kind of manure?' said the other owner, now not looking as angry as before.

'Don't ask me whether it'll act as a manure or not. All I know is that petrol isn't an oil.'

'It certainly is an oil!' said the man, now in a much better mood.

The water level was quite low now, and the oryza stalks were exposed right down to the roots, covered in red blotches that resembled burns.

'Well, I'm goin' to cut down all my plants now anyway,' said the owner with a laugh.

He and Budory then cut down every single plant at the stalk, sowed buckwheat, covered the seeds with earth and left. And just as the owner had predicted, Budory spent the entire winter eating only buckwheat. When spring came, the owner said to him …

'Budory, the number of working paddies is down this year a third compared to last year, so the work won't be nearly as tiring. So, in place of the work, I want you to study hard the books that my son who died read and figure out ways to produce a great crop of oryza that'll amaze all those people who laughed at me and called me a speculator.'

At that, he gave Budory a huge stack of all sorts of books. Budory went through them one after the other when he had time off work. The most interesting of those books were the ones with the ideas and thoughts of a man named Koobow. Budory read those books over and over, and desperately wanted to go to Ihatov City so that he could study at the school where Prof. Koobow taught a month-long course.

By the time the summer had rolled well along, Budory had distinguished himself admirably in his work for the marsh paddy owner. He stopped the disease from attacking the oryza plants as it had the year before by using wood ash and salt. By mid-August, all of the stalks were boasting fine ears, and on each and every ear a little white flower blossomed, flowers that gradually produced pale-blue grains, all of which swayed in waves with the wind. The owner, full of pride, felt triumphant.

'What do ya say?' he boasted to whoever showed up. 'I bungled the crop for four years speculating on oryza, but this year I'm takin' in four years' worth. That's about as good as it gets, wouldn't you say?'

But the year after that did not go as well. It didn't rain at all from the time of planting, the paddies dried out, cracks formed in the mud, and the autumn harvest proved barely sufficient to provide food for the winter. The owner was counting on the year after that, but the drought that year was just as bad as the previous year. Every year he counted on the next, as, little by little, he was able to afford less and less manure, sold off his horse and, eventually, let go of most of the paddies, too.

One autumn day, the owner bitterly told Budory …

'Budory, I used to be a great farmer here in Ihatov and once made myself piles of money, but because of the cold and the drought that keep coming, I own only one-third of the paddies I once did, and I haven't got any more manure left for next year. It's not only me. There's almost no one left in Ihatov who can buy manure to use. This being so, I don't know when I'd be able to pay you for the work you would do for me. I'd hate to see you wasting your best years living with me like this. I'm really sorry, but take this and go where you can to find good fortune.'

Having said that, the owner gave Budory a bag of money, a suit of clothes made of hemp dyed navy blue and a pair of red leather shoes.

Budory forgot all about how hard the work there had been and thought that he didn't need anything at all and that he just wanted to keep working.  But then he realised that there wouldn't be much work for him to do if he stayed on, so he thanked the owner profusely, parted with the man and the paddies he had known for six years and started off in the direction of the station.

## THE GREAT PROFESSOR KOOBOW

BUDORY WALKED FOR ABOUT TWO HOURS UNTIL HE CAME TO THE station.  Then he bought a ticket and boarded the train for Ihatov City. The train went ahead at full speed, rapidly leaving behind one marsh paddy after another; and the dense black woods beyond them seemed to change their shape as they receded into the distance. Budory's heart was full of many thoughts and feelings. He wanted to get to Ihatov City as soon as he could and meet the man called Koobow who had written those kind-hearted books, and, if possible, study there while working out a way to compensate for things like volcanic ash and drought and cold summers, so that all the people would be able to harvest their crop without suffering and worry ... and thinking all this made the train seem like it was just crawling along.

The train arrived at Ihatov City in the afternoon of that day. He stepped off it and lingered for a while, listening to the bubbling sounds coming up from the ground and staring at the overcast sky and standing in a daze amidst the many cars that were racing by him. He snapped out of that daze and asked people there how to get to Prof. Koobow's school.  All the people he asked simply burst out laughing at the sight of Budory's earnest face.

'Never heard of a school like that,' they said.

'Just keep walkin' another five or six blocks and ask someone again,' they said.

It was nearly evening by the time Budory found the school.

Someone was speaking in a loud voice on the first floor of that big crumbling white building.

'Hello!' shouted Budory.

No one came out.

'Hello!!' he yelled again at the very top of his lungs.

At that, a man stuck his big grey face out of the first-floor window directly above Budory. The lenses of his glasses glittered like stars.

'Quiet, will ya? There's a class going on up here! If you've come for something, get on in here,' hollered the man before pulling his head into the window, after which there was raucous laughter in the room and the man started going on about something again in the same loud voice.

Budory plucked up his nerve, entered the building and climbed the stairs to the first floor, trying to make as little noise as possible as he walked. The door at the top of the stairs was open and an enormous room appeared right before him. The room was crammed with pupils wearing all types of clothes. There was a black wall on the opposite side of the room with lots of white lines scrawled over it, and the tall man in glasses from before was pointing to various parts of a large model of a tower and explaining something loudly to the pupils.

It only took one look at the tower for Budory to realise that this was the model of what had been called in the professor's book 'The History of History'. The professor laughed, took hold of a knob and turned it. The tower model made a clicking sound and turned into a bizarrely-shaped ship. When he clicked the knob around again, the model was now transformed into the shape of a huge centipede.

All the pupils cocked their head one way then the next, utterly puzzled by what they were seeing, but to Budory it all just looked incredibly intruiging.

'This diagram will make it clear,' said the professor, nimbly drawing an elaborate diagram on the black wall.

He had chalk in his left hand too, and he also drew with that. The pupils copied everything diligently. As for Budory, he took the mud-stained little diary from his inside coat pocket that he had kept with him from the time he worked in the marsh paddies and copied down the diagram in it. The professor had finished his drawing and was now standing straight as a pin on the rostrum, glaring around the room at his pupils. Budory, too, had finished his drawing and was examining it when the pupil next to him yawned a big yawn.

'Um, what's the name of this professor?' asked Budory quietly.

The pupil chortled through his nose, as if making fun of Budory.

'He's the great Prof. Koobow,' he said. 'You really didn't know?'

The pupil looked Budory up and down, then added …

'You really think you can draw this diagram the first time around? I've been taking this same course for six years now.'

The pupil stuffed his notebook into the inside pocket of his jacket. At that moment the lights in the room flashed on. It was already evening. The great professor spoke …

'The evening is upon us, and lectures are concluded. Those amongst you who aspire to something further, you may, as is our custom, submit your notebooks for perusal, and, you will be assigned accordingly on the basis of your answers to questions put individually to you.'

The pupils gave out a yell, flapping their notebooks closed. The majority of them left just like that, but about fifty or sixty of them formed a single line in front of the professor with their notebooks open for him to examine. The professor glanced over each one, asked a question or two and wrote in chalk on their lapel, 'Pass' or 'Re-examine' or 'E for Effort'. The pupils were cringing in trepidation all the while before slipping into the corridor and shrugging their shoulders; and when they got their friends to read what the professor had written on their lapel, they either found themselves smiling in glee or frowning in misery.

The examination was soon finished, and, at last, only Budory was left. When Budory took out his little muddy diary, Prof. Koobow yawned a cavernous yawn, and, stooping down, ran an eye carefully over it. He got so close to it that it looked like he was going to swallow it up.

'Fine. This diagram is exceedingly correct,' he said, taking a deep and satisfying breath. 'But what's the meaning of all this other stuff? Ah, manure for the marsh paddies and horse feed, I see. Well, now answer me this. What are the various colours of smoke that emanate from the chimney of a factory?'

'Black, dark brown, yellow, grey, white, colourless,' burst out Budory in a clear voice. 'As well as a mixture of those.'

The great professor smiled.

'Excellent that you included 'colourless'.  Now, tell me about the shapes.'

'If there is a large amount of smoke on a windless day, it will rise straight up, with the top end gradually spreading out.  If the clouds are extremely low, the pole of smoke will rise up to the clouds, then spread to the sides. On days when the wind is blowing, the pole of smoke will rise on an angle, with its inclination determined by the extent of the wind's force.  Waves or cleavages in the smoke will depend upon the wind, as well as upon the peculiarities of the smoke and the chimney themselves.  If there is only very little smoke, it may take on the shape of a corkscrew; and if there is a heavy gas mixed into the smoke, it may come out of the chimney in the form of a tassel, then fall to the ground in one or any number of places.'

The great professor once again smiled.

'Fine.  What kind of work do you do, son?'

'I've come in search of work.'

'There's a very interesting job that needs to be done here.  Here's my name card. Go right away to the place I write on it.'

The professor produced a name card, jotted something down on it and handed it to Budory. Budory bowed and was about to go out the door when the great professor softly whispered, 'What's this? Are they burning rubbish or something?'  He then gathered up his pieces of chalk, his handkerchief and books, all of which were on the table, and threw them together into his briefcase, which he slipped under his arm, before flitting right out the very same window that he had stuck his head out before. Budory, shocked, ran to the window. The great professor was already riding in a little airship that looked like a big toy, steering it over the pale-blue mist that had enveloped the town and straight into the distance. Budory stared in amazement as the great professor landed on the flat roof of a huge grey building and connected his airship onto what looked like a hook before slipping into the building and vanishing from sight.

## THE IHATOV BUREAU OF VOLCANOS

BUDORY WENT TO THE ADDRESS THAT PROF. KOOBOW HAD WRITTEN on his name card, and there he found an imposing brown building with a tall tassel-shaped pillar in the back that loomed distinctly white against the night sky. He stood in the entry hall and pushed a button that rang a bell. A man came out immediately, took the name card, glanced over it and, on the spot, led Budory to a large room straight down the corridor.

The room had the biggest table that Budory had ever seen; and sitting up right at the middle of the table was a distinguished-looking man with a clump of white hair on his head and a telephone receiver to his ear, writing something down. The moment he caught sight of Budory, he indicated that he should sit in the chair right beside him, then turned back to his writing.

A huge model map of all Ihatov, coloured in beautiful colours, covered the entire right-hand side wall of the room, and all of the railroad tracks and towns and rivers and fields could be made out on it at a glance. A mountain range ran like a backbone straight down the middle of the map, and there was also a string of green mountains skirting the coast, with red and bitter-orange and yellow lights attached to the row of mountains that formed a scattering of islands branching out from it into the sea; and those lights changed colours, whirring like cicada, and displayed numbers that appeared and disappeared in a flash.  Well over a hundred black typewriter-like machines sat in three rows on shelves affixed to the wall below, all quietly humming away. Budory, forgetting himself, watched as the man laid down the receiver, and, reaching into his inside pocket, pulled out a name card holder.

'Are you Budory Goosko?' he asked, handing Budory his name card.  'Here's my card.'

The card read …

NOM PENPEN
Chief Engineer
Ihatov Bureau of Volcanos

When he saw that Budory, unused to the formalities of greeting, was fidgeting about, he added politely …

'Prof. Koobow phoned, so I have been expecting you. So, from now on I want you to work here and learn whatever you can. We just started up last year, but the work here carries a good deal of responsibility, and half of that comes from the fact that we're working atop a volcano and no one knows when it will erupt.  Besides, it's the very peculiar nature of volcanic eruptions that they are not really amenable to prediction. We've got to keep our wits about us. Now, you'll be staying over there tonight, so relax and have a good rest.  I'll take you around this building tomorrow.'

The next morning, Budory was given a tour of every corner of the building by Chief Engineer Penpen and shown the workings of the various machines and monitoring instruments. All of them recorded and displayed graphs and figures of the state of the three-hundred-odd active and dormant volcanos of Ihatov, those that spewed out smoke and ash and sent lava flowing down their slopes, as well as those ancient ones that looked totally inactive, indicating everything from the amount of magma and gas in them to the alterations in the shape of their mountains. The models rang out with different sounds whenever there was an abrupt change in a situation.

From that day on Budory learned how to handle all of the instruments and mechanisms and how to observe the findings, working and studying night and day, throwing himself into his work heart and soul. After two years, Budory went out with his co-workers, installing monitoring instruments in any number of volcanos and repairing those instruments that were not working properly, until he knew the three-hundred-odd volcanos of Ihatov and the ins and outs of their activity as if such knowledge was his second nature.

There were, in reality, some seventy volcanos in Ihatov that spewed out smoke and lava every day, and another fifty-odd dormant ones that expelled gas and boiling water. Among the remaining one hundred sixty or seventy extinct volcanos were those that couldn't be counted on to remain that way forever.

When Budory was working alongside Chief Engineer Penpen one day, the instrument monitoring the Sanmorini Volcano on the south coast began, without warning, to stir.

'Budory,' cried out Chief Engineer Penpen, 'Sanmorini's been pretty quiet till today, hasn't it?'

'Yes, I've not seen Sanmorini stir until now.'

'Ah, there's an eruption looming. This morning's earthquake has stirred it up. Sanmorini Township lies ten kilometres north of the mountain. An explosion now would probably knock off one-third of the mountain's northern face, sending boulders the size of cows or tables, together with fiery ash and gas, all over Sanmorini Township. We've got to drill a borehole into the side of the mountain that faces the sea to let the gas and lava out before it's too late. Let's go right now to have a look.'

The two of them got ready immediately and boarded the train bound for Sanmorini.

## THE SANMORINI VOLCANO

THE TWO OF THEM ARRIVED IN SANMORINI TOWNSHIP ON THE morning of the next day and, around noon, climbed up to the hut that housed the observation instruments near the summit of Mt. Sanmorini. The old outer rim of the crater faced the sea; and when they looked out of the window of the hut, the sea appeared like so many stripes of blue and grey, and the steamer gliding over those wavy stripes sent up plumes of black smoke as it left a silver channel in its wake.

The chief engineer calmly examined all of the monitoring instruments.

'How many days do you think it will take this mountain to erupt?' he asked Budory.

'Less than a month, I'd say, sir.'

'Less than a month? Less than ten days, I'd say. If we don't engineer this right away, there'll be no going back. It seems to me that the weakest spot on this mountain where it faces the sea is over there.'

The chief engineer pointed to a light green patch of grassland above a ravine on the slope of the mountain. The shadow of a cloud was skating easily over it, turning it from green to blue.

'There are only two layers of lava there. In addition, there's a layer of soft volcanic ash and lapilli. Besides, a great road from the stock farm leading up there means that we can transport our materials without difficulty. I'll radio the engineering brigade and call them in.'

The chief engineer began to busy himself with a call to headquarters, when there was a faint grumbling sound under their feet and the observation hut momentarily creaked and squeaked. The chief engineer moved away from the monitoring instruments.

'Headquarters are sending out the engineering brigade right away. Might be more appropriate to call them the suicide brigade. I've never been involved in any job more dangerous than this.'

'Do you think we can manage it in ten days?'

'I do. The equipment will be up here from the Sanmorini Power Plant in three days, and it'll take, I'd say, another five to string the wiring.'

He counted with his fingers while pondering something, then, appearing relieved, spoke calmly again.

'Anyway, Budory, how about brewing up some tea. The view's just so magnificent from here.'

Budory lit the alcohol lamp that they had brought with them and began to boil up some water. Clouds began to appear in the sky, and the sea had become a cheerless grey as the sun seemed to fall away and white crests rolled, one after the other, against the foot of the mountain.

All of a sudden, a weirdly shaped little airship that Budory had seen before appeared before his eyes. The chief engineer bolted up.

'Ah, Prof. Koobow's here,' he said.

Budory followed him out of the hut. The airship had already landed on top of a massive rock wall to the left of the hut, and the tall Prof. Koobow was nimbly hopping out of it. For a while he searched the area on top of the rock for a big fissure, then, finding it, promptly anchored down the airship by driving a screw into it.

'I've come for a cup of tea,' said the great professor, grinning. 'Is there a lot of trembling and shaking going on?'

'Not much yet,' answered the chief engineer. 'However, rocks are crumbling off the cliff face above here.'

It was precisely then ... the mountain groaned, as if in fury, and everything seemed to turn blue in front of Budory's eyes. The mountain was now ferociously shaking and trembling. When he looked down, he saw both Prof. Koobow and the chief engineer crouched down, clinging to the ground. The airship was pitching and rolling like a ship on waves.

When the earthquake finally ceased, Prof. Koobow stood up and dashed into the hut. The kettle had been knocked over, and the alcohol in the lamp was glowing blue. Prof. Koobow examined the monitoring instruments thoroughly, after which he entered into a long discussion with the chief engineer.

'Whatever the case may be,' he said, 'we've got to build our tidal power stations and get them working by next year. If we do that, come what may, we'll be able to take on any challenge and Budory here will have all the manure he needs to rain over his marsh paddies.'

'And he won't have to worry ever again about droughts,' said Chief Engineer Penpen.

Budory's heart leapt for joy. In fact, he thought it was dancing right up the side of the mountain! But the mountain at that moment again shook and quaked violently, and Budory was thrown to the floor.

'We can do it. We can do it!' said the great professor, adding, 'They no doubt felt that in Sanmorini Township as well.'

'What just happened now,' said the chief engineer, 'is that below our feet, about one kilometre to the north of here, seven hundred metres below the surface of the Earth, a lump of rock about sixty or seventy times the size of this hut fell into a pool of magma. But before the crust lets gas fly out of it, one or two hundred rocks like that will be holding it all inside first.'

The great professor was plunged into thought.

'Very well,' he finally said. 'I will take my leave now.'

Having said that, he left the hut and, in a flash, nimbly leapt into his airship. The chief engineer and Budory watched as the great professor waved a light in his hands two or three times in parting, circled the mountain and flew away.

Chief Engineer Penpen and Budory returned to the hut, taking turns sleeping and observing.

When, at dawn, the engineering brigade arrived at the foot of the mountain, the chief engineer left Budory alone in the hut and climbed down to the grassland that he had pointed to the day before. The voices of all the men and the clanking of the iron and steel of the materials they had brought sailed up the slopes on the wind, making it sound like they were already on the mountain.

Chief Engineer Penpen made sure that everyone was constantly informed about the progress of the work, keeping an eye all the while on the pressure of the gas and any changes in the shape of the mountain. For three days the Earth there quaked and rumbled, and neither Budory up above nor those down below could get more than a wink of sleep. The chief engineer radioed up to Budory on the morning of the fourth day.

'That Budory? We're all ready. Get yourself down here right away. Check the monitors and leave them on, and bring all your graphs with you. That hut's going to disappear from the face of the Earth this afternoon.'

Budory did exactly as he was told and descended the mountain. Huge pieces of iron and steel that had been kept in storage at headquarters had gone into making a tower, and machines were there just waiting to be wired up. Chief Engineer Penpen's cheeks were sunken in, and the faces of the engineers of the engineering brigade had turned pale. But their eyes lit up when they saw Budory, and they greeted him with big smiles.

'Well, let's pull out. Everybody get ready and hop into the cars,' said the chief engineer.

All of the engineers hurried into twenty cars that raced along the foot of the mountain in a single line toward Sanmorini Township. Just as they were about halfway between the mountain and the township, the chief engineer stopped the cars.

'Pitch your tents here, men!' he said. 'We all need some sleep.'

All of them collapsed into a deep sleep without a word of objection. The next afternoon, the chief engineer put down his radio earphones and cried out …

'The wires are in place! Budory, this is it!'

He flicked the switch. Budory and the others left their tents and gazed at a point halfway up the mountain. The meadow leading up to the mountain was blanketed in white lilies, and the peak rose above it, a majestic blue tower.

All of a sudden, the left base of the mountain swayed and quaked, and a black column of smoke emerged and rose straight up to the sky, taking on a strange mushroom-like form and giving off golden lava at its base, gleaming the moment it appeared. The lava took on a fan shape before their eyes as it flowed into the sea. Now the earth shook violently, the blanket of lilies pitched and rolled, and a thundering boom, strong enough to knock them all off their feet, hit them, with a huge gust of wind following in its wake.

'Hell yes! We've done it!' cried everyone, pointing to the mountain.

Smoke from Mt. Sanmorini spread out, breaking apart throughout the sky, the sky was soon pitch black, and hot little stones and pebbles rained down on them. They all went anxiously into the tents.

'Budory,' said Chief Engineer Penpen, 'it's gone well. The danger has completely passed. The only thing the township has to worry about now is a bit of ash falling on it.'

The little stones and pebbles soon turned into ash, then that too thinned out, and everyone rushed out of the tents. The entire meadow was now dark grey, covered by ash about three centimetres deep, all of the lilies were crushed and buried in ash, and the sky had taken on a strange green tint. A little bulge had appeared at the foot of Mt. Sanmorini, and from that a column of grey smoke was rising rapidly upwards.

That evening, all of the people climbed back up the mountain, stepping on ash, little rocks and pebbles, and, after installing new monitoring instruments, made their way back on home.


## A SEA OF CLOUDS


AS MANY AS TWO HUNDRED TIDAL POWER STATIONS WERE BUILT along the seacoast of Ihatov during the following four years, just as Prof. Koobow had planned. Observation huts and towers painted white were erected, one after the other, on the volcanos encircling Ihatov.

Budory, who now had a good grounding in engineering, spent most of his year making the rounds from volcano to volcano, fixing up equipment on those that were in danger of erupting.

In the spring of the following year, the Ihatov Bureau of Volcanos put up a poster in the villages and towns.

***Nitrogenous fertilizer to be released from the sky.***

*Ammonium nitrate will be rained upon your paddies and your vegetable fields together with the summer rains. Those people using fertilizer please compensate suitably for this in your calculations. The amount is 120 kilograms within a one hundred metre radius. We shall also be providing some rain.*

*In case of drought, we will be able to provide at least enough rain so that your crop will not die, so even those who have not planted until now due to lack of water may plant this year without the slightest qualms!*

June of the next year found Budory in the hut atop Mt. Ihatov, the volcano in the very middle of Ihatov. A grey sea of clouds spread below him. The peaks of other volcanos in and around Ihatov stood out like black islands. A single airship was flying from peak to peak right above the clouds, as if forming bridges between them, with smoke white as snow puffing from its tail. With time, the smoke gradually thickened, and its outlines sharpened as it noiselessly landed on the sea of clouds below; and, before long, there was a gigantic pale-white radiant net stretching from mountain to mountain. Having cast this net of smoke, the airship described a circle in the air, as if in greeting, and finally, with its nose angled downward, sunk easily into the clouds.

The radio earphones buzzed. It was Chief Engineer Penpen speaking.

'My airship's back safely. Everything down below is in place. It's raining cats and dogs. Now's the time. Switch it on.'

Budory pushed a button. In an instant, the net of smoke sparkled a beautiful pink and blue and purple, flickering on and off so brightly as to dazzle the eyes. Budory was spellbound by the sight. As day gave way to night and the lights in the sea of clouds went out, everything turned a shade of grey, now light, now dark.

The earphones buzzed again.

'The ammonium nitrate is all mixed in with the rain. The amount is just about right, too. The spread also seems good. Another four hours of doing this and this region will have had enough for this month. Keep doing what you're doing.'

Budory was so happy he felt like jumping for joy.

The owner of the paddies with the red beard and the man who wondered whether petrol would act as a fertilizer were listening with glee to the sound of the rain coming from the clouds. The next day they would no doubt not believe their eyes when they stroked their oryza stalks that had suddenly come up green. They gazed as if in a dream at the cloud cover that alternated between a blanket of total darkness and a sheet of soft radiance. But the short summer night seemed to be breaking, and the eastern edge of the sea of clouds shone dim and yellow amidst flashes of lightning.

It was the light of the moon, a huge yellow moon slowly rising … and when the clouds shone blue, the moon's face was strangely whitish, and when the clouds shone pink, it looked like it was smiling. Budory couldn't remember who he was or what he was doing there. All he could do was gaze blankly at what was unfolding before his eyes.

The earphones buzzed again.

'There's a lot of thunder down here. The net seems to have torn away in some places. If we keep making such a racket, tomorrow's papers are bound to give us hell, so let's call it a day for now.'

Budory put down the earphones and pricked up his ears. The sea of clouds was certainly muttering and murmuring. Listening even more intently to the sound, he could tell that it was being produced by the cracks and rolls of thunderbolts.

Budory pressed the button off. The clouds were now instantly illuminated by the light of the moon alone as they continued to sail in silence towards the north. Budory wrapped himself in his blanket and was soon lost to sleep.

## AUTUMN

IT MAY HAVE BEEN PARTIALLY DUE TO THE WEATHER, BUT THE CROP harvest that year was the best in ten years, and the Bureau of Volcanos was showered with letters of appreciation and support from every corner of Ihatov. For the first time in his life Budory felt that he had something to live for.

One day after harvest time, however, Budory was passing a little village set among paddies on his way back from a visit to Mt. Tacina. He stopped in a general store where they sold everything from soup to nuts. It was just about noon and he wanted to buy some vitamin tablets.

'Do you have tablets?' he asked.

Three barefoot men were in the store, their eyes bright red from drinking. One of them stood up.

'Yeah, we got tablets,' he said, 'but they ain't tablets you can swallow. They're tablets you write on.'

The other men ogled Budory with funny looks and burst out laughing. Budory, offended, shot outside. A tall man with a crewcut walked up to him.

'Hey, you!' he said. 'You're that Budory guy who rained down all that dung stuff with that electric thing, ain't ya?'

'That's right,' said Budory casually.

'Hey, Budory from the volcano bureau's here!' hollered the man. 'Everybody get over here!'

That brought eighteen farmers from the store and the nearby fields, all of them guffawing and roaring with laughter.

'God damn you!' said one of them. ''Cause of your stupid damn electric thing, all of our oryza plants fell down. What the hell did you think you were doin', eh?'

'Fell down? Didn't you people see the posters we put up in the spring?'

'God damn you!' said one of the men, knocking Budory's hat off his head.

They then all closed in on Budory, beating him up and stomping on him. It wasn't long before Budory was flat on the ground, unconscious.

When he came to, he was in a white bed in what looked like a hospital. There were many letters and telegrams expressing sympathy by his pillow. Budory was hurting all over, his whole body felt very hot, and he couldn't move. But a week later he was fully recovered. The paper had reported that the oryza plants had fallen down because an agricultural engineer had given the wrong instructions on how much fertilizer to use but had blamed the whole thing on the volcano bureau to cover up his blunder. When Budory read this, all he could do was laugh to himself.

The hospital caretaker visited him the next day.

'A lady by the name of Neri has come to see you,' he said.

Budory couldn't believe his ears. The next thing he knew, a tan woman looking like a farmer's wife timidly entered the room. Though she looked like a different person, it was definitely his little sister Neri who had been snatched from the house in the woods by a man. They remained silent for a time, until Budory spoke up and asked her what had happened to her after that. Speaking in her rustic Ihatov accent, Neri little by little told him everything. Three days after abducting her, the man seemed to conclude that she wasn't worth the trouble, left her at a small stock farm in the district and vanished into thin air.

She had wandered all around there bawling her eyes out, when the owner of the farm took pity on her and brought her home, putting her to work babysitting their newborn child. It wasn't long before Neri was doing various jobs around the farm, and, a few years ago, she married the farmer's eldest son. She explained that, thanks to the fertilizer that had rained down this year, they didn't have to carry dung to faraway fields like always, and they were able to use it on nearby turnip fields instead, and the corn crop that was cultivated in the faraway fields came good, and everyone in the house was very happy. She had gone any number of times with the farmer's son back to the old forest, but their house was in ruins and she didn't know where Budory had gone, and she always came back heartbroken, but because her husband had read in the newspaper the day before of how Budory had been hurt, she was able to visit him now.

Neri left, with Budory promising to go to her home to thank everyone.


## CARBONADO ISLAND

THE FOLLOWING FIVE YEARS BROUGHT ONLY HAPPINESS TO BUDORY. He often went back to the house of the man with the red beard to express thanks to him.

The man had put on some years but was still spry and full of vigour. He now bred longhair rabbits and had over a thousand of them, and he grew red kale in his fields. He hadn't given up his old speculating, but his life was better now than it had ever been.

Neri gave birth to an adorable baby boy. She dressed him up to look like a little farm boy and sometimes took him, with her husband, to Budory's house to stay overnight.

One day, a man who had worked with Budory when he was raising silkworms came to visit him with the news that his parents' grave was under an immense Japanese nutmeg tree at the very edge of the forest. At the time he had found their cold bodies when walking about the forest inspecting trees and had secretly buried them without telling Budory, placing the branch of a birch tree over the grave. Budory lost no time taking Neri there, putting up a gravestone made of white limestone. He never failed to visit the gravesite whenever he was nearby.

Budory finally turned twenty-seven. It looked as if another cold winter was about to be upon them. The people at the weather station had predicted as much that February, judging by the degree of sunlight and the condition of the ice in the northern seas. Each day confirmed this. The magnolia trees did not bloom, and May saw as many as ten days of sleet. Everyone was filled with trepidation, recalling the disastrous harvests of the past. Prof. Koobow spoke often with weather experts and agricultural engineers, writing his opinions in the newspaper, but no one knew what to do, in the end, about the approaching cold summer.

The young oryza plants were still yellow and many trees had sprouted no leaves even by the beginning of June. Budory wasn't about to take the situation lying down. If things continued in this way, there would be countless people in the forests and fields suffering the same fate that his family had suffered years before. He spent night after night plunged into thought, often not even bothering to eat. One evening, he went to see Prof. Koobow at his home.

'Professor, if the amount of carbon dioxide increases in the air, it will get warmer, won't it?'

'Yes, that's what would happen. After all, it's said that the temperature since the Earth was formed has been, by and large, determined by the amount of carbon dioxide in the air.'

'If the volcanic island of Carbonado erupted now, would there be enough carbon dioxide expelled to change the climate?'

'I've calculated that, you know. Were it to erupt now, the gas would mix into the upper air currents and circulate, until it enveloped the globe. It would prevent the diffusion of heat in the lower stratum, as well as heat emanating from the Earth's surface, thus raising the average air temperature some five degrees.'

'Professor, can we make it erupt right away?'

'We most likely can. However, the last person up there to do the job will not be able to escape.'

'Professor, let me do it! I beg you to tell Chief Engineer Penpen to give his permission.'

'There is no way that I can do that. You are still young, and there aren't many others who could do the work that you do.'

'From now on there will be lots of people like me, people who can do anything better than me, people who will accomplish their work far more brilliantly and more beautifully than I can.'

'I won't continue discussing this. Bring it up with Chief Engineer Penpen, if you wish.'

Budory left and brought up the issue with Chief Engineer Penpen.

'It's a good idea,' the chief engineer nodded. 'But I'm going to be the one who does it. I'm sixty-three this year. I'm quite content to end my life here and now.'

'Sir, but no one knows how it will turn out. It might erupt and the gas might get all soaked up by the rain. It might not go as we think. If you go up there, who will be left to figure out what to do next?'

The old engineer's head drooped down and he fell silent.

Three days after that, the volcano bureau's ship sailed rapidly for Carbonado Island. Several towers were erected on it, and the wires were connected.

When everything was ready, Budory sent everyone else back on the ship, remaining on the island all by himself.

On the next day, the people of Ihatov saw their blue sky cloud to green, and the face of both the sun and moon turn the colour of copper.

But, three or four days later, the weather became steadily warmer, and that autumn brought a harvest that was almost normal. And countless people who might have had a life just like that of Budory, Neri and their father and mother at the beginning of this story were able to pass that winter happily, with warm food on their tables and bright firewood in their hearths.

# The Frandon Agricultural School Pig

A PIG WAS GAZING UP AT THE HEAVENS ONE EVENING. HE FELT particularly happy within himself and was full of gratitude for all things given to him.

That night, first-year students, fresh from studying chemistry, stood before the pig and gazed at him in wonder. As for the pig, he threw furtive glances at them, raising his angry little eyes shaped like broad beans.

'Pigs are really bizarre little creatures,' one of the students was saying. 'They drink water and eat things like slippers and straw and turn it all into first-class fat and meat. I mean, a pig's body is, well, one big living, breathing catalyst. It's like platinum. Platinum's inorganic, so I guess a pig is its organic equivalent. The more you think about it, the weirder it gets.'

The pig, of course, heard himself being mentioned in the same breath as platinum. He knew, too, that the price of platinum was exorbitant, so he was able in a flash to calculate, with his weight of seventy-five kilograms, just about how much his body would be worth. He made this calculation folding his ears right down, closing his lids into a narrow squint and curling his front feet around.

Based on the current price of platinum, which he happened to know, he reckoned that his body was worth a good 600,000 yen. This value put him roughly in the category of what a first-class Frandon gentleman was worth. He was pretty sure of that.

It was natural, then, that he should feel a deep sense of satisfaction, seeing as he was right up there with the gentlemen of Frandon; and he opened his big mouth, in shadow resembling a shark's, smirking with joy.

However, the pig's joy did not last long.

Two or three days later, a big heap of food thudded down into his pen, and inside the heap he caught sight of a longish narrow object with thin white hairs cropped short.

This is no time for mincing words: The object was plainly a Camel Brand toothbrush.

The pig immediately felt his heart leap into his mouth. The minute he set eyes on that brush, the hairs all over his body whirred like grasses blown by the wind.

He screwed up his face, staring for a really long time at the brush, but finally felt dizzy and deeply repulsed. He immediately buried his head in the straw of his litter and was soon fast asleep, dead to the world.

The pig awoke quietly that evening and was feeling in a slightly more buoyant mood. Now, a slightly buoyant mood for a pig is in no way to be compared with the crispness of an apple or the brightness of a cloudless blue sky. We are talking pigs' moods here, so let's call it a grey mood … a grey mood that's a trifle chilly and as transparent as the wind. Having said that, you really have to be a pig yourself to fathom the feelings of a pig.

Now, exotic Yorkshire or black Berkshire pigs don't think of themselves as indolent or slow on the uptake. The hardest thing to imagine is what a pig feels when his straight back is being thrashed with a rod. Is it Japanese or Italian? German or English? It all comes out as screams. A pig's expressions, being outside the realm of our empirical knowledge, are unknowable to us.

Anyway, the pig got pudgier and pudgier, just sleeping and waking up over and over again. A teacher of animal husbandry at the Frandon Agricultural School came to the pen every day, glaring sharply at the pig and calculating its weight.

'Make sure you clamp the window down a bit tighter,' said the teacher to his young assistant, who was wearing a light-blue jacket. 'The room has to be dark for the fat to sweeten up, you know. It's high time we started really fattening this one up. I want you to start feeding him on linseed.'

The pig heard every word of this, and it really made him feel sick. It was the same feeling he felt when he saw the toothbrush. And even though he ought to have been happy being fed linseed, he simply found it hard to swallow. He knew in his gut by the tone of the teacher's voice what he was getting at.

'Those two humans feed me, but they also sometimes look at my body with a stare as cold as a polar sky and have wicked thoughts about me. Oh, I'm frightened! So frightened!'

This is what was racing through the pig's mind as, unable to hold it in any longer, he butted the fence in front of him over and over again with his snout.

However, when there was exactly a month to go before the pig was to be slaughtered, the king issued an order proclaiming the 'Law of Signed Consent Governing the Slaughtering of Farm Animals'. The proclamation stated that anyone wishing to kill a farm animal must first obtain a Certificate of Consent of Death from the animal in question. Moreover, these consent certificates must be 'signed' by the animals themselves.

So, cows and horses and all the other animals around this time were forced by their owners, on the day before they were to be slaughtered, to plop their foot or hoof or whatever down as a mark of approval of their death. The really old horses, having had their horseshoes pried off them, pressed their hoof down to seal their fate with tears flowing down their face.

The pig in Frandon got a look at a death certificate too. This happened when the principal of the Frandon Agricultural School came to him one day with a big yellow sheet of paper on which it was printed.

The pig had made a considerable study of languages, and in

addition, thanks to having a soft tongue and a natural aptitude for speech, was fluent in humanese. He greeted the principal calmly.

'Fine day we're having, isn't it, principal.'

The principal, the yellow certificate under his arm, stuffed his hands in his pockets and smiled wryly.

'Yeah, well, it's not bad,' he said.

Somehow the principal's words entered the pig's ears and formed a lump in his throat. Besides, the way the principal was ogling his body reminded him of the way that teacher of animal husbandry gazed at him.

The pig, forlorn, lowered his ears.

'I must confess I'm pretty low these days,' he said.

'Hmm. Low, eh?' said the principal, with the wry smile still on his lips. 'I see. Fed up with this world, are we?  Maybe that's the reason, eh?'

The pig had such a glum look on his face that the principal suddenly fell silent. He and the pig just stood there, staring in silence at each other. They stood their ground, not a word passing between them. Finally, the principal spoke …

'So, anyway, you have a good rest,' he said, deciding to give up on the certificate for that day. 'And don't move about a lot, okay?'

The principal left with the big yellow certificate firmly under his arm.

After that, the pig went over and over the words of the principal in his mind, thinking about his wry smile and his ulterior motive.  He trembled and said to himself …

'…"So, anyway, you have a good rest. And don't move about a lot, okay?" What on earth does he mean by that?  Oh, I can't cope with this.  I just can't!'

These were the thoughts going through his trapezoidal head and splitting it with pain. That night there was a huge blizzard, and outside, as the winds raged, fragments of dry snow blew in through cracks in the shed where the pig lived, turning what was left of his food pure white.

However, the next day, the animal husbandry teacher came again, leading that same red-faced assistant in the light-blue jacket. He looked daggers at the pig, a look that virtually devoured him from his head and ears to his back and tail.

'You're giving it linseed every day, I hope,' he said, with one pointy finger in the air.

'Yes, I am,' answered the assistant.

'Thought so. We'll settle for tomorrow or day after tomorrow. We've gotta get the approval certificate over with. I wonder what happened. I'm sure the principal came in here with the certificate under his arm.'

'Yes, sir, apparently he did.'

'Well, then, I guess he's already got what we need. He should have passed it on to us, by all rights.'

'Yes, sir.'

'Why don't we make this room a bit darker than it is. And also, the day before we do the thing, don't give it any feed.'

'No, sir, I don't plan to.'

The teacher of animal husbandry threw another sharp glance at the pig, glared at him for a moment, then left the shed.

Once again, words went splitting through the pig's head, and he was overwhelmed by anguish.

'What does he mean by "approval certificate"?' he thought. 'What kind of approval certificate? They say they're not going to feed me the day before. But, the day before what? What on earth does he want me to do? What on earth is he going to do to me? Is he going to take me far away and sell me? Oh, I can't cope with this. I just can't!'

The pig couldn't sleep well at all that night due to frazzled nerves. However, the next morning, when the sun was finally up, three students, boarders at the school, entered the shed, cackling away. Once again, the pig, who had slept badly all night and whose head was wracked with pain, was forced to hear a most unwelcome conversation.

'When are they going to get it over with? I can't wait to see it.'

'Not me.  I don't want to watch it.'

'I just want it to be soon. The leeks in storage will freeze if they're left there much longer.'

'The potatoes are there too.'

'There are over fifty kilos in storage. There's no way we can get through that much by ourselves.'

'It's freezing today too,' said one of the students, blowing white breath onto his hands.

'Yeah, but the pig looks pretty warm.'

The three of them burst out into a raucous laugh. 'The pig's got his fat an' it's just like he's wearin' a three-centimetre thick overcoat, so he's warm as toast.'

'Yeah, toast.  You said it. He's so warm he's givin' off steam.'

The pig was so sad hearing this that it took all his strength just to totter onto his feet.

'The animal should be finished off right now.'

The three students left the shed, whispering to each other. Once they were gone, the pig's thoughts once again agonised him.

'…"I want to see it done now … I don't want to watch … the leeks are freezing … over fifty kilos of potatoes … we can't eat them all … an overcoat of fat three-centimetres thick…." Oh, this is horrible. They look right through you. Horrible, horrible! But, what on earth do a bunch of leeks have to do with me? Oh, I can't cope with this. I just can't!'

Just then, while the pig was in agony, the principal returned to the shed. He slapped the snow off himself and, with that ambiguous wry smile on his lips, stood before the pig.

'So, how're we feeling today?' he asked. 'Feeling happier?'

'Yes, sir, thank you very much.'

'Happier, are you? That's marvellous. Enjoying your food?'

'Thank you very much. It's perfectly fine.'

'Fine, is it? Good to hear it. Now, actually, I've come today to have a very confidential talk with you. Your head's clear, isn't it?'

'It is,' answered the pig with a bit of a frog in his throat.

'Well, in actuality, every creature on this Earth has to die someday. Every single living thing actually dies. Even the nobility among humans, the rich, and also middle-class people like me and even the most worthless beggars, die.'

'I see,' said the pig, his voice sticking in his throat and not coming out very clearly.

'And, you see, even animals that are not human, for example, horses and cows and chickens, and even catfish and even bacteria … they all have to die. The mayfly that is born with the rising of tomorrow's sun dies in the evening. A life that lasts only a single day. Everything's gotta die. Take me and you. It's our fate to die someday too.'

'I see.'

The pig couldn't say anything more than that for the frog in his throat.

'So, now comes the thing I want to talk to you about. We here at the school have looked after you up to today. I'm not boasting here, but the school has done a pretty good job taking care of you. Other pigs like you are scattered all over the place, and, well, I'm very aware of this … and, uh, it may sound funny but, uh, there's no place where animals are treated better than right here.'

'Yes, sir.'

This is what the pig wanted to say, but the food that he had eaten before was now a big lump in his throat, and no words could come out.

'So, anyway, this is what I came to talk about. If, uh, you have, because of all this treatment … if you have even a tiny bit of gratitude in you, I've got a teeny favour to ask, I mean, to ask for your permission.'

'I see.'

Again, the lump in his throat was preventing him from answering.

'It's really just a teeny-weeny thing. See this sheet of paper here? This is what's written on it. "Certificate of Consent of Death. I, long enjoying your solid patronage and as it suits you, do hereby accede to dying. Day month year, at Frandon Sheds. To the Principal of the Frandon Agricultural School, Yorkshire." That's all it says.'

Having said this, the principal went in for the kill.

'What it means is that you're going to die sooner or later, so now you can die gracefully, I mean, you're ready to die at any moment and that it's really no big deal. No one at all would need to die if their time wasn't up. So, I just need you to give me your front legs and for you to put your hoofprint on this. That's the long and short of it.'

The pig knit his brow and carefully read the certificate that the principal was holding before him. If what the principal was saying was true, this 'no big deal' was something absolutely terrifying. Finally, the pig spoke through his tears, doing his best to control himself.

'If one can die at any time, are you saying that that time should be today?'

The principal was taken aback, but soon regained his composure.

'Well, yes. But, it absolutely doesn't have to be today. No.'

'Then, are you saying it will be tomorrow?'

'Well, uh, tomorrow … nobody's saying it has to be that soon. Whenever … sometime. It's really a vague sort of thing.'

'When you say I'll be dying, does it mean that I will be dying naturally?' asked the pig, again in a shrill voice.

'Yeah, well, no, that's not what we're looking at here.'

'No, I won't. I won't! I refuse to do this. I absolutely refuse,' the pig screamed, weeping.

'You refuse? Then our hands are tied. You are really so ungrateful! You're even lower than a dog or a cat!'

The principal shoved the certificate in his pocket and, taking big strides, stormed out of the shed, his face bright red from anger.

'I'm lower than a dog or a cat from the beginning, anyway, so what's the difference? Waaaah!'

He couldn't stop weeping and wailing as the bitter disappointment and sadness welled up in him. But, after a half day of weeping and wailing like that, the tiredness that he felt from not sleeping for two nights overcame him and, with tears still flowing down his cheeks, he was lost to sleep. Even while asleep, however, his legs shook and trembled over and over again from fear.

The next day dawned, and that same teacher, with his assistant in tow, arrived again. And again with that highly disturbing look in his eyes, he glared at the pig and spoke to his assistant. He was obviously in a filthy mood.

'What's going on here, eh? The weight's obviously not going up. Even a farmer can get a pig to this weight. What's happening here, eh? Got any idea?  Look at those hollow cheeks, will ya? And get a load of that shoulder, will ya? Got no flesh on it.  Wouldn't stand a chance in a show competition. What the hell's goin' on here, eh?!'

The assistant put his finger to his lip and thought for a moment.

'Well, the principal was here yesterday afternoon,' he said. 'Perhaps that's it.'

The teacher of animal husbandry gave a start.

'The principal? I see. The principal. He no doubt came to get the pig's approval and bungled it royally. He gave the thing the willies, that's what. So, the thing has been goin' round and round the pen and hasn't slept a wink all night. This is a revolting turn of events. And, what's worse, he's no doubt bungled the certificate. Revolting, positively revolting.'

The teacher grit his teeth in disappointment, making a grinding sound, and folded his arms over his chest.

'Well, there's nothing to do about it. Open up the window all the way. Then, take the thing out and give it some exercise. Beat the animal mercilessly and make it run and run. Then walk it on the grassy area, where there's no snow, in the shadow of the stables, which doesn't get much sun. Fifteen minutes at a time. Then don't feed it. Make it a bit hungry. When it calms down, give it a little of the soft part of a cabbage. Then, when it gets better, go back to the old routine. A whole month of fattening it up has gone down the drain in a single night.

Do I make myself clear?'

'Yes, sir. I will do it.'

The teacher went back to the staff common room, and the pig calmed down considerably. He didn't feel like moving or screaming. All he wanted to do was stare at the far wall of the shed. Just then, the assistant, who had gone out, returned grinning, holding a thin whip in his hand. He opened the pen's gate.

'How about a little walk, my friend?' he said, in the politest of voices. 'It's a beautiful day out there, with almost no wind to speak of. Please allow me to accompany you.'

The whip came down with a loud whistle on the pig's back. The pain was unbearable. The pig could do nothing but walk sluggishly out of his pen. His heart was overflowing with sadness, and a fierce pain was piercing his body with every step he took. The assistant followed from behind with a carefree gait, whistling 'It's a Long Way to Tipperary' while swinging his dangling whip.

'Where does he get this "Long Way to Tipperary" when I'm so filled with sadness?'

That's what the pig thought, screwing up his mouth.

'I wonder if you could possibly be bothered to walk a little more to your left,' said the assistant.

The tone of his voice was exceedingly sweet, but he brought the whip down on the pig when he spoke.

'This life is so hard, so unbearable,' thought the pig. 'This world is truly one of pain and suffering.'

He continued to walk while being severely beaten, with those thoughts rushing through his mind.

'Well now, would you care to take a rest about now?' said the assistant, bringing the whip down on the pig with great force.

The pig was forced to return to the shed, where he plopped down on his side in the straw. The assistant brought him a morsel of the delicious part of a young cabbage. The pig didn't feel like eating it, but the assistant was standing up straight with an indescribably ferocious look in his eyes, waiting for him to eat. He had no choice, so he put a small amount in his mouth and pretended to chew until the assistant, apparently mollified, sighed once, then, smiling and whistling 'It's a Long Way to Tipperary', left. The window had been left wide open from before, forcing the pig to endure the unbearable cold.

In this way the pig spent three days as if in a dream, sunk into depression. On the fourth day, the teacher of animal husbandry came once again with his assistant. The teacher threw a single glance at the pig.

'This will not do, definitely not do!' he said to his assistant, waving a hand. 'Why didn't you do what I told you to?'

'I did. I opened the window all the way and gave the thing the good part of a cabbage. I exercised it carefully every day, fifteen minutes at a time.'

'Did you? I'm surprised you didn't get a result if you really did that. Well, the thing is just getting skinnier and skinnier. Neurotic undernourishment, that's what's the problem. We've got to do something before it becomes a bag of skin and bones. I don't think we'll succeed like this. Look, close all the windows. We'll forcefeed the thing mechanically and shove food down into it. Get three and a half kilos of wheat bran and about four hundred grams of linseed, and also about a kilo of corn meal. Mix it all with about a litre of water and make dumplings out of it.'

The teacher continued ...

'Put them in the forcefeeder and feed that amount to the thing in two or three portions a day. We have a forcefeeding apparatus, don't we?'

'Yes, sir, we do.'

'Tie the thing up now. No, before tying it up, we've got to get it to consent to its death. The principal really bungled things up royally, didn't he.'

The teacher of animal husbandry hurried off in the direction of the classroom building, followed by his assistant.

Not long after that, the principal arrived in a great huff and puff. The pig, with no place to lie down, had dug a hole in his litter with his snout.

'Listen here. We're running out of time. I've got the Certificate of Consent of Death here again. You've really got to put your hoof down on it today. It's no big deal. Come on, give it your hoof.'

'I won't. I refuse,' said the pig, sobbing.

'You refuse? Listen here. Stop thinking only of yourself. You have that body of yours thanks to the efforts of everybody at this school. From today we're going to give you three and a half kilos of wheat bran, four hundred grams of linseed, and a kilo of cornmeal every day. So, come off your high horse and give us your hoof. Come on, we've no time to lose.'

The principal looked very ferocious when he got angry like that, and the pig was petrified.

'I will. I'll do it,' he said, in a hoarse voice.

'Good. Very well,' said the principal, now in good spirits.

He produced the yellow sheet of paper on which the Certificate of Consent of Death was printed, and spread it before the pig.

'Where do I put my hoofprint?' asked the pig in tears.

'Right here. Just under your name,' said the principal, looking at the pig's little eyes through his glasses.

The pig nervously screwed up his mouth to one side, lifted his short right front hoof in trepidation and brought it down on the spot.

'Ah, excellent. This is smashing,' said the principal, now in a superb mood, pulling the sheet of paper to him and examining the mark.

The mean-spirited teacher of animal husbandry, who had been waiting in the doorway, suddenly entered.

'How's it going? Did it go well?'

'Yep. We've got it. Well, then, I'll just give this to you. So, how many days of forcefeeding will there be?'

'Well, we'll keep an eye on it and monitor the situation. Chickens and ducks fatten up without any problem, but a pig who's a nervous wreck like this one might not fatten up through forcefeeding so easily.'

'Oh, right. I see. Be that as it may, give it your best shot.'

With that, the principal left. It wasn't long before the assistant showed up carrying a funny-looking canvas tube with screws sticking out of it and a bucket of something. At the instruction of the teacher of animal husbandry, the assistant put his hand in the bucket, checking its contents by picking some of it up in his fingers.

'Right. So, now tie the pig up.'

The assistant rushed into the pen with a hemp rope in his hands. The pig put up a good struggle, but eventually found himself in the corner of his pen with his two right legs tied to two iron rings.

'Smashing. Now put this end down its throat,' said the teacher of animal husbandry, passing the canvas tube to his assistant.

'Now, open your mouth. Come on, open up,' said the assistant calmly.

But the pig kept his mouth shut tight, clamping his teeth together.

'We've no choice. Put this between its teeth.'

The teacher handed the assistant a short steel pipe. The assistant squeezed the pipe in between the pig's teeth. The pig roared and cried at the top of his voice, but the tube was eventually forced between his teeth. Now he could cry only at the base of his throat. The assistant pushed the canvas tube into the space made by the steel pipe and down the pig's throat.

'Excellent. Now, let's get started.'

The teacher piped the food in the bucket into the end of the canvas tube, and, with the help of a weirdly-shaped spiral, sent it down into the pig's stomach. No matter how hard the pig tried not to swallow, he couldn't stop the food from getting past his throat. The dumplings went down into his stomach, making him feel very heavy and full. This, after all, is what forcefeeding is all about.

The pig felt so awful that he wept uncontrollably for an entire day. The teacher came back to have a look the next day.

'Well done. It's fatter. This has produced an effect. I want you and the caretaker to continue to feed it, two times a day each.'

And so, for seven days from that time on, the pig saw neither the light of day nor felt the wind in his face. All he knew was that his stomach was getting oppressively heavy and that his cheeks and flanks were becoming so bloated that every breath he took was a chore in itself. The students took turns coming into the shed, discussing various matters in front of him. One day ten of them showed up, gabbing away like this …

'It's really gotten fat. I wonder how many kilos the thing weighs.'

'Well, the teacher says he can tell at a single glance, but it's tough for us to do the same.'

'We don't know its specific gravity, that's why.'

'I know the specific gravity, if it's specific gravity you're talking about. It's pretty much the same as water.'

'How do you know that?'

'Because that's what it is, roughly. If you put the thing in water, it wouldn't sink, but it wouldn't float either.'

'Nope, it wouldn't sink. It'd float for sure.'

'That's because of the fat. But pigs have bones too. And they have meat on them. I'd bet that its specific gravity would be just about one.'

'So, if the thing's specific gravity is about one, then how much would it weigh?'

'About a hundred kilos, I'd say.'

'Rubbish. It wouldn't be a hundred. It'd be at least a hundred and thirty.'

'No, it'd go over a hundred and thirty. Closer to a hundred and fifty for sure.'

'Well, let's settle for a hundred and forty. A litre of water weighs a kilogram, so it would weigh in at a hundred and forty kilos.'

'Gosh, a hundred and forty kilos!'

The pig simply cried his eyes out upon hearing all this. It was just too much for him.

They're measuring someone's body as they would merchandise … a hundred and thirty kilos, a hundred and forty kilos.

On the seventh day, the teacher and his assistant once again stood side by side in front of the pig.

'It looks fine now. Just right. This degree of fattening is just what the doctor ordered. Couldn't be sweeter, I'd say. If you fatten them up too much, they get sick on you and you lose precious time. Tomorrow would be ideal, I'd say. Don't feed it any more today. And wash the thing thoroughly with the caretaker. And change its litter. Got it?'

'Yes, sir.  Will be done.'

The pig had pricked up its ears and listened intently to what the two men were saying.

'So, it's to be tomorrow,' he thought. 'It's because of that death consent certificate. Tomorrow and tomorrow and tomorrow. Oh, what's going to happen to me? I can't cope with this.'

The pig was in such agony that he butted his head hard against the planks of the pen.

The assistant returned that afternoon together with the caretaker. They freed the pig from the iron rings.

'How are we today?' said the assistant. 'Today we're having a nice little bath. It's all ready and waiting for you.'

Before the pig could nod or say a word, the whip cracked down hard on his back. He had no choice but to start walking.  But because he was so fat, even a single move was exhausting, and he was panting after taking only three steps.

The whip came cracking down again. The pig was on his last legs, but managed finally to walk out of the animal shed, where there was a huge wooden basin filled with hot water.

'Go on in now,' said the assistant, cracking the whip on the pig's back.

With great difficulty the pig rolled over the tall top edge of the basin and into the water. The caretaker washed the pig clean using a large brush. But the pig shrieked its head off when he saw the brush; for, after all, the brush's bristles were made of pig's hair. While he was shrieking, his body turned pure white.

'Now, let's be on our way, shall we?' said the assistant, bringing his whip down on the pig with stinging force.

The pig could do nothing but get out of the water. The cold bit into every part of his body, and he let out a big sneeze.

'It'll catch its death,' said the caretaker, with eyes like saucers.

'So what? Its meat won't go off,' said the assistant, sneering.

The pig returned to the shed, where new straw had been laid out in his pen. Little blades of cold cut through him. He hadn't eaten since the day before, and his empty tummy was growling and rumbling like thunder. His eyes were closed.  His head rang with pain. The entire life of this pig, with its many terrifying memories, went through his head, flickering like the flame of a stone lantern in the garden. He heard all sorts of horrifying noises in his head. He couldn't even tell if they were ringing outside or inside him.

The morning bell in the classroom building would be ringing by now. That moment, a babble of voices could be heard, and a big group of students came into the shed. Amongst them was the assistant.

'Shall we do it outside? I think outside is best. Take the thing outside. Hey, I said take it outside and I don't want to hear any whining! It just takes the shine off everything.'

The teacher of animal husbandry was standing in the doorway, dressed this time in a brown gown-like coat.

'And how are we now?' said the assistant, entering the pen. 'It appears to be a lovely day outside.' Bringing the whip down onto the pig's back, he added, 'Would you care for a little stroll today?'

The pig, without any protest whatsoever, swelled up his cheeks, gasped for breath, and hobbled out. He was completely knackered. The two black legs of each student moved forward and to the side as if in a dream.

Suddenly it was blindingly light. The pig walked listlessly, squinting his eyes at the brightness of sun shining off the snow.

'Where on earth are they taking me?'

There was a single cedar tree in the distance. The pig flicked its head up and suddenly saw an intense white light flash, scattering sparks throughout the sky before his eyes. Countless red flames shot out to the sides like spouts of water. A sharp metallic sound rang through the heavens. A torrent of water gushed out on all sides....

What happened after that I cannot say. Right beside the pig stood the teacher of animal husbandry breathing hard, his face a trifle pale, a huge iron sledgehammer in his hands. The pig lay at his feet. It twice let out a high-pitched purr from its nose, then ceased to move.

The students were a hive of activity. They washed the pig's body in the basin, then changed the water, rolled up the sleeves of their coats as high as they could and stood by patiently. The assistant thrust a large jackknife deep into the pig's throat.

THIS STORY IS SO FULL OF MISERY, I THINK I'LL LEAVE IT HERE. Be that as it may, the pig was soon cut into eight slabs which were piled one atop the other behind the stables, then buried in the snow for a night to keep them fresh.

That night the sky was crystal clear. Taurus the Bull, with its silver horns, came out sparkling, and a crescent moon, shining coldly, poured its light, like pale mercury, over the clouds. And buried, piled on its bed of snow like bodies in a battlefield cemetery, was the body of the pig, washed clean and sliced into eight pieces.

The moon passed over in silence. The cold night was, at last, as crisp as it can be.

# Snow Crossing

The snow was frozen stiff, even more solid than marble, and, to all appearances, the sky was a cold smooth blue sheet of stone.

*Packed Snow, Cold Snow, Crunch and ... Slip!*

The sun burned a pure white, releasing the fragrance of lily all about, glittering the snow below. As for the trees, they were dazzling, decked in a frost of what looked like icing sugar.

*Packed Snow, Cold Snow, Crunch and ... Slip!*

Shiro and Kanko went kicking and gliding into the fields in their little straw boots. Who could imagine a more fun day than this? They could go as far as they chose, over the meadows blanketed in pampas grass and through the millet fields which they couldn't always cross.

The plain was like a single sheet. And it glittered and glistened like so many tiny little mirrors.

*Packed Snow, Cold Snow, Crunch and ... Slip!*

The two children approached the forest. The body of a huge oak tree was bending from the weight of icicles embedded in it, hanging down splendorous and transparent. The two of them cried out at the top of their lungs, facing the forest.

*Packed Snow, Cold Snow, Crunch and … Slip! The little fox, he wants a bride, he does, he does!*

For a time it was as quiet as a whisper, and when the two of them held their breath to cry out once more, the little white fox came out of the forest, padding over the creaking snow, saying …

*Cold Snow, Slippery-slippery, Packed Snow, Squeak and Creak!*

Shiro, slightly taken aback, shielded Kanko behind him, stood his ground and cried out …

*Yelpy Fox, Icy Fox, if you want a bride, you'll have one!*

At that, the fox—though just a little slip of a fox—tweaked his taut silver needle-like whiskers, and said …

*Slippery Shiro, Crunchy Kanko, as for me I need no bride!*

Shiro laughed and said …

*Yelpy Fox, Little Fox, if you don't need a bride then have some rice cakes instead!*

At that the little fox, shaking his head twice and thrice, merrily said …

*Slippery Shiro, Crunchy Kanko, want my millet dumplings instead?*

Kanko, hiding behind Shiro's back, was so tickled by this that she softly sang …

*Yelpy Fox, Little Fox, your dumplings are made of rabbit poo!*

At that Konzaburo the Little Fox chuckled and said …

*Oh no, that's absolutely wrong. Would fine upstanding humans like you ever consume things like brown rabbit dumplings? Up till now we have been falsely accused, I swear, of pulling the wool over the eyes of humans.*

Shiro, surprised, asked the fox …

*You mean, it's a lie about foxes outfoxing people?*

Konzaburo answered earnestly …

*Indubitably. Arguably the most unfair lie that ever was. The people who claim to be outfoxed by us are usually drunk or so chicken-hearted that they've gone bananas. You wouldn't believe it. Take Jinbei.  Little while ago, on a moonlit night, he sat himself down in front of our house and sang traditional joruri ballads till late at night.  Brought us all out for a look, it did.*

Shiro cried out …

*Jinbei wouldn't be singing traditional joruri ballads. It must have been traditional naniwabushi ballads!*

Konzaburo seemed to agree with this …

*Yeah, you might be right. Anyway, have yourselves some dumplings. These dumplings of mine are the result of my diligently preparing the land, sowing the seeds, weeding the weeds, reaping, thrashing, making the flour, kneading the dough, steaming and sugaring them.  How about it?  Would you like a plateful?*

Shiro laughed …

*My dear Konzaburo. We have only just eaten rice cakes now and are not in the least hungry.  We'll take a rain check on these, if we may.*

Konzaburo the Little Fox was pleased.  He waved his short arms and said …

*If you wish. In any case, you can have some at the Magic Lantern Party. You wouldn't miss the Magic Lantern Party, would you? We'll meet on the evening of the next moonlit night when the snow freezes over. We start at eight, and I'll give you your admission tickets now. How many would you like?*

*Well, we'll take five then.*

*Five? That's two for you two, but who are the other three for?*

*Our elder brothers.*

*Are they eleven or under?*

*No, the youngest is in year four, and four plus eight makes twelve.*

At that, Konzaburo tweaked his whiskers like before, adding with a serious air …

*In that event, I regret to inform you that your elder brothers may not attend. Just you come.  I'll set aside reserve seats for you.  You'll have the time of your life.*

*The first slide takes up 'Thou Shalt Not Drink' and it shows Taemon and Seisaku from your village who, having drunk themselves blue in the face, are just about to eat these funny buns and buckwheat noodles in the field. I'm in the photograph too.*

*The second one is entitled 'Thou Shalt Be Wary Of Traps' and it depicts one of our number, Konbei, caught in a trap in a field. It's a picture. It's not a photograph.*

*The third is called 'Thou Shalt Not Make Light Of Fire' and it shows a scene of one of our number, Konsuke, scorching his tail at your house. We'll be expecting you.*

Most pleased, the two children nodded. The fox turned up the corner of his mouth as if highly amused himself, began to kick and tap, kick and tap his feet, then shook his tail and head in thought, finally appeared to have hit upon an idea and sang out in rhythm, waving both paws in the air …

*Cold Snow, Packed Snow, Slip and Crunch*

   *The Buns in the Field are Puffy Puff Puff*

*Tipsy and Tottering is Good Ol' Taemon*

   *Last year He Ate a Good Thirty-Eight Buns!*

*Cold Snow, Packed Snow, Slip and Crunch*

   *The Noodles in the Field are Fluffy Fluff Fluff*

*Tipsy and Tottering is Good Ol' Seisaku*

   *Last Year He Ate Thirteen Bowls Full!*

Both Shiro and Kanko were carried away by the song, dancing in concert with the fox.

*Kick kick tap tap … kick kick tap tap … kick kick kick kick … tap tap tap!*

Shiro sang out …

*Yelpy Fox, Little Fox, just last year Konbei the fox stuck his foot in a trap. Yelp yelp thump thump … yelp yelp yelp!*

Kanko sang out …

*Yelpy Fox, Little Fox, just last year Konsuke the fox picked a fish off the fire, burning his behind. Yap yap yap!*

*Kick tap tap … kick kick tap tap … kick kick kick kick … tap tap tap!*

The three of them danced their way, step by step, into the woods.

The wind stirred the new red magnolia leaves, fashioned of sealing wax, causing them to flash in spurts, the indigo shadows of the trees spread their huge net onto the snow in the woods … and it looked as if silver lilies were blooming where the rays of the sun struck the ground.

At that, Konzaburo the Little Fox said …

*Should we ask the fawn to come here too? The little deer's so good at the flute.*

Shiro and Kanko clapped their hands in delight, and the three of them cried out in unison …

*Packed Snow, Cold Snow, Crunch and Slip. The little deer, he wants a bride, he does, he does!*

Then they heard a fine thin voice coming from the distance …

*The north wind goes peep, it's Saburo of the Wind. The west wind goes roar, it's Matasaburo again.*

Konzaburo the Little Fox pouted his lips mockingly, saying …

*That's the fawn. He's much too timid to ever come over to us. But why don't we call to him once more?*

The three of them cried out again …

*Packed Snow, Cold Snow, Crunch and Slip. The little deer, he wants a bride, he does, he does!*

From far far away they heard what sounded like the wind or a flute or, perhaps, a fawn's song …

*The north wind goes peep, too cold to sleep*

*The west wind goes roar, knocks on my door*

The fox tweaked his whiskers again and said …

*We can't wait till the snow gets all soft, so go on home now. Come again, won't you, when the snow freezes over on a moonlit night. We'll do the magic lantern I told you about.*

Shiro and Kanko sang out …

*Packed Snow, Cold Snow, Crunch and Slip*

They crossed over the silvery snow toward home.

*Packed Snow, Cold Snow, Crunch and Slip!*

*

AN ENORMOUS PALE FULL MOON ROSE SLOWLY OVER ICE MOUNTAIN. The snow gleamed blue in its light and, once again today, froze solid like a slab of white marble.

Shiro recalled his promise to Konzaburo the Little Fox and said softly to his little sister, Kanko …

*Tonight's the foxes' Magic Lantern Party. Should we go to it?*

At that, Kanko jumped up and cried out …

*Yes, let's. We should. Yelpy Fox, Little Fox, Yelpy Konzaburo the Fox!*

Then Jiro, the second oldest brother, said …

*Are you two going to visit the fox? I want to go too.*

Shiro shrugged his shoulders at a loss for what to do, saying …

*Oh, Jiro. But the foxes' Magic Lantern Party is only for children up to eleven. That's what it says on the ticket.*

Jiro replied …

*What ticket? Lemme see. Uh-huh. 'We beg to inform you that save for the immediate family of the school's pupils no one twelve or over will be permitted entrance.' Boy, these foxes sure are professional. I can't go, I guess. Can't be helped. But if you're going, take some rice cakes for them with you. Here, these mirror-shaped ones are just the thing.*

Shiro and Kanko put on their little straw boots and went out carrying the rice cakes. Ichiro, the eldest brother, Jiro the second and Saburo the third stood side by side in the doorway.

*Bye-bye. If you meet up with an adult fox, be sure to shut your eyes right away. Now we'll sing for you. Packed Snow, Cold Snow, Crunch and Slip. The little fox he wants a bride, he does, he does!*

And the moon rose high in the sky and the forest was shrouded in pale smoke. The two children arrived at the entrance to the forest. A little white baby fox, with an acorn badge pinned to his chest, was standing there …

*Good evening. Good morning. Do you have a ticket?*

*We do.*

The two of them showed their tickets.

*Well then, this way please.*

The baby fox leaned forward formally and, winking and blinking all the while, indicated a point inside the forest with his paw. The moonlight shone down as if hurled on an angle into the forest like any number of bolts of blue. The children came to a clearing in the forest. There they saw lots of pupils from Fox Elementary School already gathered, throwing chestnut shells at each other, practicing sumo … and the funniest thing of all was the teeny-weeny little fox, no bigger than a mouse, riding piggyback on the large young fox while trying to reach for the stars.

A white sheet was hanging from the branch of a tree in front of them. Out of the blue they heard a voice behind them …

*Good evening. So nice of you to come. It was a pleasure seeing you the other day.*

Shiro and Kanko turned about in surprise to see Konzaburo before them. Konzaburo, sporting an elegant swallow-tail coat and a narcissus on his chest, was busily wiping his pointy mouth with a snow-white handkerchief.

Shiro, bowing slightly, said …

*The pleasure's all ours. And also, thank you for tonight. These rice cakes are for all of you to eat.*

All of the pupils at Fox Elementary School were staring at them. Konzaburo puffed his chest fully out and proudly received the rice cakes.

*I cannot thank you enough for this gift. Please make yourselves every bit at home. The magic lantern show will begin in two shakes of a lamb's tail. Now, if you will excuse me …*

Konzaburo left them, taking the rice cakes with him. The pupils at Fox Elementary School cried out in unison …

*Packed Snow, Cold Snow, Crunch and Slip. Hard rice cakes will crack your snout … white rice cakes will slither about!*

A large sign appeared next to the curtain.

RECEIVED: ONE PILE OF RICE CAKES FROM MASTER SHIRO, HUMAN BEING AND MISS KANKO, ALSO HUMAN BEING

The fox pupils clapped their paws in glee. At that moment, a whistle whistled. Konzaburo cleared his throat with two 'ahems' as he appeared to one side of the curtain, bowing politely.

This quieted everyone down.

*We have superb weather tonight. The moon may as well be a plate made of pearls. The stars appear to be dew on the meadow fixed in permanent twinkling. Now it's time for the Magic Lantern Party. I ask all of you to open your eyes as wide as you can and refrain from blinking and sneezing. Furthermore, I request that you all remain silent this evening in deference to our two honoured guests. There will be no tossing of chestnut shells in their direction. This concludes my opening remarks.*

They all clapped their paws in glee. Then Shiro said quietly to Kanko …

*Konzaburo really knows his stuff, doesn't he.*

The whistle whistled again, and THOU SHALT NOT DRINK was projected onto the screen in large type. Then that was replaced with a photograph. It depicted a drunk old human male with his hands around some funny round object. They all stamped their feet and sang out …

*Kick kick tap tap, kick kick tap tap*

*Cold Snow, Packed Snow, Slip and Crunch*

*The Buns in the Field are Puffy Puff Puff*

*Tipsy and Tottering is Good Ol' Taemon*

*Last Year He Ate a Good Thirty-Eight Buns!*

*Kick kick kick kick, tap tap tap!*

The photograph disappeared.  Shiro said softly to Kanko …

*That's Konzaburo's song.*

Another photograph came on. A young drunk human was eating something with his head buried in a bowl-like object made of a magnolia leaf. Konzaburo was watching in the distance wearing a white hakama. They all stamped their feet and sang out …

*Kick kick tap tap, kick kick tap tap*

   *Cold Snow, Packed Snow, Slip and Crunch*

      *The Noodles in the Field are Fluffy Fluff Fluff*

      *Tipsy and Tottering is Good Ol' Seisaku*

      *Last Year He Ate Thirteen Bowls Full!*

*Kick kick kick kick, tap tap tap!*

The photograph went off and a short interval followed. An adorable little vixen came around with two plates of millet dumplings. Shiro was at a complete loss for what to do. This was because he had just seen Taemon and Seisaku eating something bad without realising it. In addition, all the pupils at Fox Elementary School were turned towards them, whispering amongst themselves …

*Will they eat one?  What do you think, will they eat one?*

Kanko just held a plate in her hand, blushing bashfully from ear to ear. At that, Shiro made up his mind and said …

*It's all right. Let's eat them. Come on, eat up. I don't really think Konzaburo is pulling a fast one on us.*

The two of them ate up all the millet dumplings. They tasted like heaven. The pupils at Fox Elementary School jumped for joy and danced about …

*Kick kick tap tap, kick kick tap tap*

*By day the sun beats down its light*

*By night the moon is blue and bright*

*Break their bones and let them die*

*No fox pupil would ever lie*

*Kick kick tap tap, kick kick tap tap*

*By day the sun beats down its light*

*By night the moon is blue and bright*

*Push them down in snow and hail*

*No fox pupil would ever steal*

*Kick kick tap tap, kick kick tap tap*

*By day the sun beats down its light*

*By night the moon is blue and bright*

*Tear them from their fathers and mothers*

*No fox pupil would envy others*

*Kick kick tap tap, kick kick tap tap*

Shiro and Kanko wept for sheer joy. The whistle whistled, THOU SHALT NOT MAKE LIGHT OF TRAPS appeared on the sheet in large lettering before it was replaced by a picture. This one pictured Konbei the fox with his left foot caught in a trap.

*Yelpy Fox, Little Fox, just last year Konbei the fox stuck his foot in a trap.*

*Yelp yelp thump thump, yelp yelp yelp!*

That's what they all sang.  Shiro said softly to Kanko …

*That's the song I made up.*

The picture was replaced with the words THOU SHALT NOT MAKE LIGHT OF FIRE, then that disappeared and another picture came on. It showed Konsuke the fox getting his tail on fire by reaching for a grilled fish. All of the fox pupils cried out …

*Yelpy Fox, Little Fox, just last year Konsuke the fox picked a fish off the fire, burning his behind. Yap yap yap!*

The whistle whistled, the curtain lit up and once again Konzaburo appeared and said …

*Well, everyone, that concludes tonight's magic lantern show. There is something that you all must truly take to heart tonight, and that is the fact that two children, who are human beings, both clever and not in the least drunk, have been kind enough to eat food made by foxes. I believe that in the future you, as adults, will neither tell lies nor be envious of others, and that the bad reputation we foxes have had up till now will be a thing of the past. This concludes my closing remarks.*

The pupils were moved, down to the last fox, raising both paws and rushing to their feet. Their cheeks glittered in tears. Konzaburo came to the two children and bowed politely, saying ...

*Well, this is goodbye.  I am eternally grateful to you for tonight.*

The two of them also bowed and went on their way towards home. The fox pupils caught up with them and filled all their pockets with acorns and chestnuts and phosphorescent stones.

*Here, these are for you.*

*Here, please have these.*

This is what they said before departing like the wind itself. Konzaburo watched with a smile on his lips.

The two children left the forest and started across the field. When they reached the very middle of that field of the palest snow, they caught sight of three dark shadows approaching them from a distance. The shadows belonged to their elder brothers who were coming for them.

# The Nighthawk Star

THE NIGHTHAWK IS TRULY AN UGLY BIRD. HIS FACE IS BLOTCHY IN spots, as if splattered with miso, and his flat beak is split right up to his ears. He can barely totter the length of a small room on those legs of his, and other birds get totally disgusted at the mere sight of his face.

For instance, the skylark isn't exactly what you would call a pretty bird, but it considers itself head and shoulders above the nighthawk. When it comes across the nighthawk in the evening, it clamps its eyelids shut and looks the other way, as if it will have nothing to do with him. The littler chatty birds just jump at the chance to say bad things to the nighthawk right under his beak.

'Humph. Here he comes again. Just look at that. He really gives us birds a bad name.'

'Yeah, I mean, have you ever seen a mouth that big? He must be related to frogs or something.'

That's the sort of thing they say. Oh, if the nighthawk was not a nighthawk but just a plain hawk instead, those shallow little birds would just shake and quiver at the mere sound of his name. They would go pale as ghosts, shrivel up into little balls and hide in the shade of some leafy tree.

But the fact of the matter is, the nighthawk is no brother to the hawk. He's not even related. He's really the big brother of that beautiful kingfisher and that jewel of a bird, the hummingbird. The hummingbird drinks nectar from flowers and the kingfisher eats fish, while the nighthawk lives off bird lice. And even the weakest birds aren't really afraid of the nighthawk, because his claws and beak are not in the least bit sharp.

This being the case, it might seem odd that there is a 'hawk' in the nighthawk's name. Yet, for one thing, the nighthawk's wings are uncannily strong, and when he soars, cutting the wind, he looks just like a hawk. For another, his cry pierces the sky. So it's not so odd, after all, that he's called a  hawk.

Now, it goes without saying that the hawk didn't let this pass it by. In fact, it didn't like it one bit. And because of this, whenever it caught sight of the nighthawk, it peered at him, bristled up its shoulders and said, 'You dump that name and get yourself a new one!'

One evening, the hawk finally went to the nighthawk's house.

'Hey, you in there?  Still have the same old name, do ya? You've got a lot of nerve, you shameless little bird. You and I aren't birds of a feather, you know. Take me. I can fly  through the blue sky to the ends of the earth. Now, take you. You only come out at night or on some dim cloudy day. Now take a good look at my beak and talons and compare them with your own, and you'll see what I mean.'

'Mr. Hawk.  It's asking too much of me to change my name. I had no hand in getting it in the first place. It came to me from heaven.'

'Whadda ya talkin' about, eh? You could say that I got my name from heaven, but your name is just borrowed from mine and the night's. Now, give it back!'

'Mr. Hawk. It's beyond me to do that.'

'Beyond you? Rubbish. I'll give you a nice name, okay? You'll be called Ichizo. Ichizo, got it? Pretty good name, eh?  And, when you change your name, you've got to make an official name-changing announcement. Okay? So, listen. You're gonna hang a name tag with ICHIZO written on it around your neck. Then you're gonna go around bowing to all the birds where they live and announce yourself by saying, From now on, I shall be known as Ichizo.'

'There's no way in the world I could do that.'

'Rubbish. You can. And you will. If you haven't done it by the morning of the day after tomorrow, I'll rip you to shreds with my talons before you know what's hit you. Keep that in mind, being clawed to death. On the morning of the day after tomorrow, I will go around from one bird's place to another and ask if you've been there or not. If there's even a single place you haven't been to, consider yourself dead as a dodo.'

'But … don't you think that's a bit overdoing it? I'd rather die than have to do all that.  Please do away with me right now.'

'Well, why don't you sleep on it, okay? I mean, what's so bad about Ichizo, eh?  Sounds like a pretty good name to me.'

The hawk spread its wings fully out and flew back home to its nest.

The nighthawk shuts his eyes, plunged in thought.

'Why on earth does everybody hate me like this so much? It's because I look like I have miso splattered over my face and my beak is split up to my ears. But I've never ever done a bad thing to anybody. When the little baby white-eye fell from its  nest, I saved it and took it back. And the white-eye tore the chick right away from me as if it was taking it back from some kind of robber or something. And then it just cackled right in my face. And now I have to go around hanging a tag around my neck saying my name's Ichizo. That's the last straw, if you ask me.'

The day turned dim and gloomy as the nighthawk alighted from his nest and flew off into the low-lying clouds. He flew about the sky without making a sound, scraping clouds that glowed with a menacing light.

Then suddenly the nighthawk opened his mouth wide, stretched his wings straight as straight can be, and shot across the sky like an arrow. Bird louse after bird louse flowed into his throat. No sooner was he about to plunge into the earth than did  he spring easily right up back to the sky. The clouds had turned  all grey, and the distant mountains were a fiery red.

When the nighthawk took to flying like that, it seemed like the very sky was split in two. A beetle who got caught in his throat started to wriggle and writhe for dear life. The nighthawk swallowed the beetle right down, but for some reason soon felt shivers up and down his spine.

The clouds were now pitch black, reflecting the fiery red of the mountains just in the east. It was terrifying. The nighthawk set out once again for the sky, choked with emotion.

Just then one more beetle got into his throat, flapping away as if bent on scratching it from the inside. The nighthawk forced the beetle down, but this just choked him up all the more; and he wept, crying out at the top of his lungs. And as he wept, he circled round and round and round the sky.

'Ah, little beetle, every night I kill many bird lice. Now the hawk is going to kill me, and there's just one of me. It's so hard to swallow. Ah, I can't take it. I can't cope any longer. I'm going to stop eating insects and starve to death. But, before that, the hawk will probably do away with me. But, before that, I'm going to go far and far away, beyond the sky.'

The flames of light on the mountains gradually spread, flowing like water through the clouds and lighting them a fiery red.

The nighthawk made a beeline for the home of his little brother, the kingfisher. The lovely kingfisher had just awakened and was gazing at the flaming light on the distant mountains.

'Good evening, big brother,' he said, watching the nighthawk descend. 'What brings you here out of the blue?'

'Uh, it's just that I'm on my way to a faraway place. I came to see you before, that's all.'

'No, you can't go! The hummingbird is already so far away, and I'll be left all by myself.'

'Well, yeah. You see, there's nothing I can do about that. Just let things be. And, by the way, from now on, I don't want you taking any fish just for fun. Only when you really need to. Well, goodbye now.'

'What's the matter? No, just wait a little bit longer.'

'No, there's no difference whether I go now or later. Please don't forget to remember me to the hummingbird. Goodbye. We won't meet again. Goodbye now.'

The nighthawk wept as he returned to his home. The short summer night was already coming to an end. Fern fronds swayed in the cold blue light, sucking in the dawn mist. The nighthawk cried out in a high-pitched screech, then, having put his nest in order and having properly preened all his feathers, once again flew away.

The mist lifted, and the sun rose exactly from the east. The nighthawk flew straight towards it like an arrow, wobbling in the air from the blinding light.

'Oh, Sun, Mr. Sun. Please take me to you. I don't mind if I die in flames. Even an ugly body like mine will give off a little light when it burns. I beg you, please take me to you.'

But no matter how far he flew, the nighthawk got no closer to the sun. On the contrary, the sun seemed to be getting farther and farther away.

'You're the nighthawk, aren't you,' said the sun. 'I see. It must be pretty hard for you. Now, go and fly around the sky and ask the same thing of the stars. When you come down to it, you're not a daylight bird.'

The nighthawk gave a bow and, in a flash, spiralled down onto the grass of a meadow. What happened after that was like out of a dream. His body was streaming high up amongst red and yellow stars, taken by the wind for what seemed like forever, as if the hawk had come and was gripping him in its talons.

Without warning, something cold fell on the nighthawk's face, and he opened his eyes. Dew was dripping from a single young stalk of pampas grass. Night had fallen, the air was giving off a pale light, and stars were twinkling from one horizon to the other. The nighthawk took off for the sky. As before, the fiery mountains were a brilliant red. The nighthawk flew amidst the dim reflection coming off the fiery-red mountains and the cold light of the stars. It flew once around the sky again, then set its sights straight for the beautiful stars of Orion in the western sky, calling out as it flew towards them.

'Oh, Stars, pale stars of the West. Please, I beg you, take me to you. I don't mind if I die in flames.'

Orion the Hunter gave the nighthawk the cold shoulder, not interrupting his brave old song. The nighthawk got all teary and tottered down, until he got ahold of himself and started to fly around the sky again. He then flew in a straight line for the Great Dog Star in the south, crying into the night.

'Oh, Star, great blue star of the South. Please, I beg you, take me to you. I don't mind if I die in flames.'

'Come off it, will ya?' said the Great Dog, twinkling and blinking its beautiful stars in blues and purples and yellows. 'Who on earth do you think you are anyway? Just a birdbrain, that's what. It would take you billions and trillions and zillions of years to reach here on those wings of yours.'

And having said that, the Great Dog Star turned its back on him.

The nighthawk spiralled down, crestfallen, until he once again circled the sky, now aiming straight for the Great Bear in  the north, crying out as he flew.

'Oh, Great Bear, blue star of the North. Please take me to you.'

'You must have your head in the clouds,' said the Great Bear calmly. 'I think you better cool off that head of yours. Now, there's nothing like plunging into a sea floating with icebergs to get your head cooled off. And if there's no sea in the vicinity, diving into a glass of ice water will do the trick just fine.'

This sent the nighthawk, dejected once again, into a tailspin, until he started to fly round and round the sky once more. Now he set out for the Eagle on the far bank of the Milky Way that had just begun to rise in the east.

'Oh, Eagle, white star of the East,' he cried. 'I beg of you, please take me to you. I don't mind if I die in flames.'

'Stop pulling my leg,' bellowed the Eagle, arrogantly. 'Not on your life. To be a star, you must have the appropriate status,  not to mention a considerable amount of money.'

This took the wind right out of the nighthawk's wings, which closed on him and sent him sailing downwards. His frail legs were no more than a foot from the ground when he rocketed up like a flare. When he had reached a place near the middle of the sky, he gave his body a shake and bristled up his feathers, just like when an eagle does attacking a bear. He then cried out in the highest piercing pitch. He sounded just like a hawk. All of the birds asleep in the meadows and forests woke up and, quailing and quaking, looked up to the starry sky, wondering what in heaven's name could be behind that sound.

The nighthawk flew on forever and ever, straight up into the sky. The fiery-red mountains were now no bigger than the tip of a cigarette. The nighthawk just climbed and climbed and climbed.

His breath froze white on his chest from the cold. And because the air was getting thinner and thinner, he had to flap his wings all the more. And yet, the stars looked no bigger than they did before. Each breath went in and out like the air in bellows. The cold and frost stabbed into him like little swords, and his wings became numb all over. He then looked up at the sky with tears in his eyes.

This was his final moment. Whether he was falling at that moment or climbing, whether upside down or right side up, he couldn't tell. But for all that, his heart was at ease, and his big bloodstained beak was bent to one side, clearly smiling a little.

It wasn't long after that that the nighthawk opened his eyes wide and saw that his body was burning quietly, giving off an exquisite phosphorescent blue light. Beside him sat Cassiopeia, and just in back of him flowed the pale light of the Milky Way.

The Nighthawk Star didn't stop burning. It continued to burn on and on and on. It burns like that to this very day.

# Translator's Afterword

In the more than fifty years that I have been reading and translating the stories and poems of Kenji Miyazawa, my passion for and sheer enjoyment of his writing have never waned. I have also watched, over this time, his reputation grow in Japan from that of a 'writer of fantasy tales for children' to that of Japan's greatest twentieth-century poet. It is certain that no other Japanese author enjoys the wide popularity—in age, gender and geographical spread —that he does in Japan today.

He was born in 1896 in the small town of Hanamaki, in Iwate prefecture, and died there in 1933. As such, his life spanned Japan's greatest growth in its economy and stature as a world power in its entire history until then. Though it was an era of unbridled nationalism, Kenji (he is referred to generally by his given name) never mentions his country's status. The words 'Japan' and 'Japanese' appear in his writing very rarely. In fact, many of the characters in his stories bear foreign names. This alone has set him apart from every other major Japanese author.

His great classic is *Night on the Milky Way Train*, the first story in this collection. It tells of two boys, Giovanni and Campanella, best friends, who find themselves on a train traversing the heavens. This trip constitutes a metaphor for loss and the overcoming of grief. Kenji was a devout Buddhist and believer that people's greatest joy came from their sacrifices for others.

In another story, *The Life of Budory Goosko*, one of Kenji's more autobiographical tales—at least from the standpoint of his inner life and his aspirations—the hero says this, shortly before giving up his life for the welfare of others …

*From now on there will be lots of people like me, people who can do anything better than me, people who will accomplish their work far more brilliantly and more beautifully than I can.*

Clearly, Kenji, in all his writings, had his eye on those who would come after him, providing them with a guide on how to work for the benefit of people around the world.

Amongst the stories here are some of his most popular, such as *The Restaurant of Many Orders*, *Gauche, the Cellist* and *The Nighthawk Star*. But I have included some others, less widely read in Japan, such as *The Frandon Agricultural School Pig*, a story about animal cruelty written nearly a century ago; and *Obbel and the Elephant*, a tale that takes up human and animal exploitation. *Snow Crossing* shows us how much we can learn from animals. Some stories are simply exquisitely told: *The Magnolia Tree* and *Indra's Net*, two prose-poems in which Kenji confronts a timeless and infinite universe.

We finally seem to be catching up, in our concerns and our ardour for new ways to relate to nature, with his themes and messages.

In so many ways, Kenji Miyazawa was a twenty-first-century author born in the nineteenth century, a supernova that exploded in 1933. The light may be just reaching us now.

*Roger Pulvers*
*2020*

www.ingramcontent.com/pod-product-compliance
Lightning Source LLC
Chambersburg PA
CBHW030633190726
48286CB00008B/2511